In Pursuit of Liberty

by Susan Brunn Puett

PublishAmerica

Baltimore

First printing

ISBN: 1-4137-2468-X
PUBLISHED BY PUBLISHAMERICA, LLLP
www.publishamerica.com
Baltimore

Printed in the United States of America

To Dave who has shared my journey,
with my love and thanks

Acknowledgments

From the time I was very young, members of both sides of my family spoke with animation about our ancestors and what was known of their lives. For sparking that interest in me and helping me visualize myself in our genealogical continuum, I will always be appreciative. Specifically, I wish to thank my mother, Margaret Brunn; my father, David Brunn; my uncle, Robert Birdsall; and my grandparents, Grace and Willard Birdsall.

Lending moral support and encouragement to this project were, most importantly, my husband Dave; my children David and Michael (his computer expertise was invaluable); my daughter-in-law, Mary; and my sister and brother-in-law, Barbara and Bob Hughes.

Lastly, I am indebted to PublishAmerica for seeing the merit in this endeavor. It is hoped that its publication will give my grandchildren, Brannon, Connor, and Meg, some of that same interest in our personal history that was my family's legacy to me.

Table of Contents

Foreword

The letters in this volume are part of a collection of material saved by James Stott's wife, Hannah, my great great great grandmother. They were kept by their eldest daughter, also named Hannah. After she married James Birdsall, they moved to a home in Seelyville, Pennsylvania. There, for the next three generations, the family remained. When the Birdsall home was eventually sold, a Stott descendant, Mary Hackley, was in possession of the memorabilia. Realizing their historical significance, she organized and transcribed portions of the letters. Following her death, all of the original material passed to my grandfather, Willard James Birdsall, then to my uncle, Robert Birdsall, and finally to me. In addition to the letters, there are sketches and essays written by James, his surveying and mathematics books, and a crossstitch done by his daughter Hannah in 1820.

For correspondence that was mailed without envelopes, sent on ships from America to England and eventually brought back to the United States, the condition of the pages is remarkably good. There are, however, in a few places words that have faded or been torn away. Those unreadable spaces are noted in italics wherever they occur. Occasionally, James utilized English words not in common usage today and also referred to events and to prominent people who played a part in the history of that period. In those instances, where needed for clarification, I have inserted numbered footnotes at the conclusion of each letter, again in italics. When James introduced footnoted explanations, they are denoted alphabetically.

The letters have been transcribed exactly as they were written with two exceptions. Presumably in an attempt to put as many words as possible in the space available, James did not use paragraphs. For ease of reading, I decided to take the liberty of inserting breaks where deemed suitable. Also, James used little in the way of punctuation. In general, commas and dashes were utilized to indicate sentence breaks. On occasion, I added periods for clarity. For the most part, the letters are beautifully composed. Although there are some words that have different spellings from those in use today and there are a few obvious errors such as repeated words, I did not correct or edit the writing in any way. What may sometimes appear to the reader to be typographical errors are, in actuality, accurate reproductions of James' presentation.

Finally, I am grateful to my ancestors for saving this small piece of history. To look at the world through their eyes has been a special gift to me. It is hoped that others will enjoy this glimpse into the life of an immigrant family.

Susan Brunn Puett

Introduction

Through monthly letters written during the three-year period from April 29, 1820 until May 15, 1823, we read, in the words of James Stott and his family, descriptions of their experiences during a time of upheaval and change.

Eloquently, the Stotts shared their impressions and responses to their new circumstances. Although the packet of letters includes correspondence from various members of the Stott family, we have nothing from James' wife, Hannah. Her reactions to James' absence and the impact of the subsequent events can only be surmised by her actions and James' comments.

This journey to America was made by many, but was uniquely personal to each who embarked upon it. About most we know little, from the Stotts we learn much.

Chapter I
The Departure

One can only imagine the tension in the Stott household as James became more and more convinced that he must flee authorities after his actions as a reformer, protesting the intolerable conditions of workers and the lack of representation for the people in Lancashire and rural England. Finally, after his participation in the now infamous 1819 Manchester meeting in St. Peter's Field which resulted in the death of eleven persons, the injuring of hundreds, and the imprisonment of others (Palmer 447), James evidently decided that the only way to insure his freedom and the safety of his family was to board a ship bound for the United States. For the protection of his friends and family, he appears to have told no one, including his wife. His letter announcing his departure was delivered ashore by the harbor pilot after James was indeed already aboard the *Lady Gallatin*[1] and under sail.

Hannah, James' wife, was seven months pregnant with their seventh surviving child (one having died in 1812 at the age of six). She was left to deal with the authorities, care for her children, and give birth without the support of James.

The saga begins with James' first fateful letter.

LETTER ONE

Liverpool Ap. 29, 1820

Dear and Loving Wife/
This is Saturday evening. Tomorrow I am going on board a Vessel now lying in the river bound to and cleared out for the City of New York - you know I have a predilection for the County in England which bears the name.[1] I trust you will bear my short absence with all that Fortitude you have hitherto displayed - be not deluded or dismayed by the flatteries or threats of men who may come to you with pretended Demands against me - say I have appointed a proper person to pay every legal Debt which I owe on my own account and that he will call and satisfy all just Claims as soon as he has collected sufficient for that Purpose - in respect to Debts owing by the Executors of the late Charles Hill, say you cannot and will not interfere, but refer them to Messrs. Bridge and Korrecks of Bury - if any inquiry is made after the Accounts say truly, as you well may, that you know nothing of them - keep your Money - make yourself and our children as happy as you can - don't spoil James - expect to hear from me as often as I have the opportunity of writing - and depend upon seeing me as soon as the Business which caused my Departure is properly arranged - Kiss my Children and bless them in my name - In true faith Love and respect I am Dearest Wife,
Your Affectionate husband
James Stott

Love to all Friends

P.S. respects to Brother William Mr. Brettargh brings a Warrant for him from me - excuse this scribble of my steel pen -

Note written along the left hand margin of the page:
W. H. Knowles will call frequently to see you - keep up your spirits don't injure your Health and hurt the peace of our children by fretting - be cautious and circumspect in all Things - speak not all that you know -

Letter addressed to:
Mrs. James Stott
Pendleton
per favor of Mr. J. Brettargh

¹Hannah was born in Yorkshire.

England in the early Nineteeth Century

During the latter part of the Eighteenth Century, Parliamentary reforms came close to being adopted in England, but by 1815 Great Britain was reacting against the French Revolution which gave rise to Napoleon and the resulting Napoleonic Wars. The idea, proclaimed by the Age of Enlightenment, that through reason, progress, and natural law, man could be free of hardships and develop a perfect society became suspect (Brinton 49).

Following the Napoleonic Wars, Great Britain had become a world industrial leader and, in addition, was in the midst of a population explosion. (The number of people in Great Britain and Ireland climbed from approximately 10,000,000 in 1750 to 30,000,000 in 1850.) This growth was mainly in the northern areas, where towns such as Manchester lacked urban political structures with no uniform ways in which to collect taxes for vital services such as sewers, police, and garbage disposal (Palmer 426-427). Protective tariffs enacted by the landed classes resulted in skyrocketing prices for basic food (Palmer 446). Poor conditions and long hours in the factories, combined with low pay and an inadequate living environment (Palmer 428), led workers to engage in sporadic, but ever increasing numbers of protests (Brinton 224). William Cobbett had started the reformist publication, *Weekly Political Register*, in 1802. By 1816, in order to interest the working class, he decided to distribute the paper at a lower cost (Nattrass xii) utilizing more colloquial vocabulary while maintaining enough sophistication to retain his middle class readership (Nattrass 135). Cobbett was credited with diverting much of the working class from the practice of engaging in random outbursts to partaking in more organized protests urging Parliamentary reform (Trevelyan 186).

At the same time, the middle class was experiencing many frustrations, including a lack of control over its own political destiny. Members of the middle class had little opportunity for voice in governmental policy. Cities such as Manchester and Birmingham had no representatives in the House of Commons. Added to that was the discrimination, in terms of holding public office, against people who did not belong to the Church of England. Since many of the new members of the industrial class were non-Anglicans, they were doubly disenfranchised (Brinton 196-7). Thus both the working and the middle classes felt they had grounds for protest.

Outbreaks of demonstrations for reform in Lancashire and Yorkshire occurred in the spring of 1817, but they were largely ineffective. A series of arrests practically eliminated any radical reform organizations that had existed in Lancashire. At that time the Seditious Meetings Bill passed, which made democratic societies and meetings illegal. Further, the suspension of the Habeas Corpus Act was extended (Halevy 26-27). This meant that no one was protected from illegal detention or imprisonment and led William Cobbett, previously jailed for two years for his radical writings, to flee temporarily to America (Trevelyan 187-188). During a reform meeting in Birch Middleton in 1818, radical William Benbow urged people to march on London. Shortly thereafter, he too decided to sail from

Liverpool to America (Bamford 125). In 1818 there was an abnormal period of prosperity, but that was followed by over-production and falling prices.

While renewed hard times began in the industrial areas of the country, in London British Foreign Minister Lord Castlereagh was maintaining that the country was experiencing favorable economic conditions (Halevy 54-56). As 1819 dawned, agitation for reform began finally to take on a coherent and spreading popularity (Edwards 42).

This then was the England in which James Stott and his family resided. James served as a civil and mining engineer to the Duke of Bridgewater, and he also conducted a private day school near Worsley in Lancashire. Born in 1778, two years after the United States declared its independence, James' entire early life was spent during the years in which democracy became an increasingly pressing topic. By his own words, James was an avid reformer and advocate for the victory of freedom from the oppression that gripped his country. Wrote James, "See the fruits of war - Maddening Debt - deadening Taxes - starving Corn Bill[2] - palsied trade - dying People and prostrate Liberty. Oh Liberty! where is thy voice now, is it lost for Ever? Will thou not arise as the bright Sun in his Strength, and dispel the purple mists of Tyranny and oppression; will our Sons be Slaves? Confound the base Soul that entertains the Thought!" (Stott, *On Liberty - A Fragment,* 1820) . Whether James used similar words at public gatherings is not known, but he was said to have been giving a lecture protesting unfair taxation of the poor when his employers decided to raid the meeting hall. James was hurried out the back of the building just moments before the Duke of Bridgewater's men arrived on the scene (Undocumented family correspondence from a Stott descendant).

Public about his reformist view, it was not until James' participation in the Manchester demonstration of 1819 that he began to become increasingly alarmed about his personal safety and that of his family. Industrialists in Manchester were determined to push forth their desire for representation in Parliament. Initially, they had decided to "elect" Henry Hunt as a Parliamentary representative. However, after a similar mock election was attempted in Birmingham, resulting in the arrest of the "winning candidate" Charles Wolseley and other principal organizers, the Manchester protest plan was altered. Industrialists, together with the distressed working class, arranged a massive reform meeting in St. Peter's Field for mid-August over which "Orator" Hunt would preside, but not stand for "election" (Halevy 63).

Estimates of between 60,000 (Trevelyan 189) and 80,000 people gathered on August 16th and called for not only the repeal of the more oppressive legislative acts, but also for annual elections to the House of Commons and universal male suffrage (Palmer 447). Rather than arrest Hunt before the meeting, authorities decided to send in yeomanry to apprehend him as he spoke. The yeomen became overwhelmed by the crowd, panicked, and began striking people with their sabers. At that point, the 15th Hussars came to the yeomen's assistance and the crowd began to flee in terror (Edwards 45). According to eyewitness radical reformer Samuel Bamford, "...then was a rush, heavy and resistless as a headlong sea; and a sound like low thunder, with screams, prayers, and imprecations from the crowd-moiled, and sabre-doomed, who could not escape. (...)Women, white-vested maids, and tender youths, were indiscriminately sabred or trampled..." (Bamford 152). By most accounts, eleven people were killed and hundreds wounded, including a hundred and thirteen women. Radicals dubbed the tragic event the "Peterloo Massacre," disdainfully comparing it to the Battle of Waterloo and, incredibly, the government publicly thanked the troops for their bravery in maintaining order (Palmer 447). James, as far as we know, was unhurt.

In reaction to the Manchester meeting, Parliament passed the Six Acts which restricted the freedom of the press, outlawed "seditious and blasphemous" literature, allowed for the search of private homes for arms, and restricted the right to hold public meetings. When a group of revolutionaries plotted to assassinate all members of the Cabinet in protest, they were apprehended on Cato Street in London, and five were hanged. Pamphleteer Richard Carlisle was sentenced to prison for publishing the works of Thomas Paine (Palmer 447), and in March of 1820, for his participation in the Manchester meeting,

Henry Hunt was given a two-and-a-half year jail term in Ilchester jail (Read 153). With reformers imprisoned, prohibitions initiated,[3] and his views common knowledge to the authorities, James decided to follow the route William Cobbett, William Benbow, and others had taken earlier—that of temporary exile from the country until the climate for reform improved and the threat of arrest was no longer a reality.

On April 30th, he sailed.

Notes for Chapter One

[1] *James Stott appears on the Passenger List of the Lady Gallatin. His age is listed as forty-two and his occupation as land surveyor (Microfiche film 0002246, Family History Library, Salt Lake City, Utah).*

[2] *The Corn Bill of 1815 was enacted raising protective tariffs on imported grains. While these acts initially benefited the farmers and landlords, the laborers became burdened by escalating prices on grain based foods (Palmer 446). When in 1820, the cost of food stuffs experienced a sudden fall resulting in increased prosperity for the working class, it spelled ruin for many farmers and landlords (Halevy 107-108). Along with Universal Suffrage and annual Parliaments, repeal of the Corn Laws became one of the most important demands of the Radical Reformers (Read 42).*

[3] *Some evidence exists that James may have been a member of the Society of Friends. In various letters, he discussed Friends Meetings and in one piece of family correspondence Hannah was referred to as a "Quakeress." After the Manchester Meeting, many religious communities including the Anglicans, Wesleyan Methodists, and Roman Catholics adopted policies of "loyalty," taking positions opposed to the Radical agitation. The official*

stand of the Quakers was to distance themselves from Radical Reformers within their organization, also choosing to accept a policy of prudent loyalty (Read 201-204). If, indeed, James was one of the Reformers within the Quaker community, the stand taken by the Friends could have been another reason for him to consider departure.

Chapter II
Exploring America

New York City in 1820

The New York City that James found upon his arrival in America had a population of 123,706 (Rosenwaike 16). Because the overwhelming influx of European immigrants was just beginning, the city was still mainly populated by native Americans, with only eleven percent having been born elsewhere (Lankevich 70). In 1820, New York did have dirty and crowded streets and docks. The prevalence of disease prompted the Board of Health to urge New Yorkers to be vaccinated against smallpox in 1815, and yellow fever epidemics occurred in both 1819 and 1822 (Lankevich 63-64). However, the drastic impact of the millions of immigrants upon Manhattan was at its very early stage. As a result, James found few of the problems that befell the arriving people in the years after 1825. The dreadful living conditions and poverty were not part of the New York of James' experience.

The signing of the Treaty of Ghent, which ended the War of 1812, was followed by a significant recession. By 1820, between 15 and 20 percent of the population of New York was receiving public assistance. The decline in the economy was short lived, however, and trade began to once again expand. Ship builders worked rapidly to fill the demand for faster ships. In 1819, the steam-driven *Savannah* made its maiden voyage to Liverpool and although sailing ships remained in use for many years thereafter, the eventual change to steamships was on the horizon. Insurance and banking, necessary for the growth of commerce and once dominated by England, was finding a place in the New York economy. The New York Board of Underwriters was started in 1820 (Lankevich 61-62).

The buying and selling of real estate in New York's rapidly expanding city made fortunes for those with money to invest. Although Boston and Philadelphia could still claim to be centers of culture and intellectual life, New York began to challenge them. St. Patrick's Cathedral was opened in 1815; the Free School Society made education available to those unable to afford private schooling; the Mercantile Library Association and the Apprentice Library were established to make books available for those with only moderate incomes; and New York City was well on its way to becoming the literary capital of America. Leading artists were living and working in New York, and the theater had begun to flourish in what would become a magnet for the performing arts (Lankevich 63-65). Thus, James landed in a New York that was dynamic, growing, and filled with much for the first time visitor to absorb.

The Beginning of James' Stay in America

The day after the *Lady Gallatin* docked in New York, James wrote his first lengthy letter announcing safe arrival. It was filled with observations that flowed rapidly, jumping quickly from one topic to the next. He divided his letter into two sections, one to be read and shared with friends and a second, more private part, meant for his family. In the first we are told about the New York City that greeted him, some of his impressions of the American people, and what little he was able to surmise concerning the availability of goods. It was in the section of the letter directed to his family that James wrote of his affection for his wife and each of their children, much about his fellow passengers on the *Lady Gallatin*, brief notes concerning his days at sea, and warnings, again, to his family about the importance of saying little concerning his activities.

Meanwhile, Hannah, remaining in England and having been advised by James to speak to no one about "all that she knows," had heard nothing about his voyage and would not until almost three months had passed. The arrival of James' first letter did not occur until well after the birth of Joseph on July 3, 1820. For his part, James was equally uninformed about the well-being of his wife and children and if, indeed, the newborn and Hannah survived the delivery. It is interesting to note that James' mention of the birthing was very obliquely referred to as "your trying and difficult situation" from which he expressed his "hope and trust in God you will get well out of Bed again."

LETTER TWO

N. York. June 23, 1820

Dear & Loving Wife /
This 23rd. of June, 1820, I sit down to inform thee that I am at Length safely arrived at New York, - I went on board the Lady Gallatin on Sunday the last Day of April and Landed in the forenoon of Yesterday, consequently was 53 compleat Days on board - before dinner I took a walk to see the City, but the weather being so intensely hot, I was much fatigued before I had seen one fourth part of it. I counted the Steeples of about twenty Churches this

Day when I was upon Long Island - the city Hall where Justice is, or ought to be, administered, is a fine Building, indeed it is Beautiful; near to it is the City of New York Museum, and not far from thence, the Washington Arms Hotel, which faces Broadway, the longest and straightest and broadest Street in the City - I walked along it about half a mile, and came to the Fire. I should have told thee before, that when we approached the City in the Night, it appeared in flames - the furious Element had now nearly spent its strength, the Engines had ceased to play, as the devouring Flames had destroyed to vacant space on every side - The ruins were smothering, and the Front wall of two Houses was standing, and some inward Walls of wood were blazing rapidly - The fire-men pushed down the Walls with a long ladder - they fell with a terrific crash amid blazing ruins - at this time thirty-two Houses were burned to the Ground. This Morning we were alarmed again by the Fire Bell - it happily proved to be only the Ruins that had broken out afresh, and which were soon gotten under.

Wednesday was the first hot Day there has been in this Country this Summer, yesterday the Thermometer stood at 95 degrees, to day has been hot, hot, but not so suffocating as yesterday, which showed much for Thunder.

This Day I have been over the East River onto Long Island, to view the city of Nassau and The Dock Yard - there is just launched one of the finest Vessels I ever saw, a three Decker, which will carry from 108 to 120 Guns; it is said to be the Longest upon the Keel, the best built, and the handsomest Vessel in the World - its length is 165 feet between Decks - it has been built by a Scotsman, it certainly is the most beautiful ship I ever saw; between Decks looks almost large enough to hold a little village; the Stern of the Vessel is adorned with the Bust of the Great Hercules, most beautifully carved, shewing Defiance in his Eyes; over his Shoulders hangs the Skin of the Nemean Lion.

We then went on Board the Washington, a well built 74, which is now laid up in ordinary - we were very complaisantly shewn through her, the Cabbins, State Rooms and all, by one of her Lieutenants; every part of her was admirably clean and regular. I forgot to say, above, that the name of the new Ship (which is the pride of Columbus), is "the Ohio" she is called after one of the Western States.

Notwithstanding the various stories you have heard about the haughtiness of the Americans, I assure you I have met with nothing but the greatest civility during the short time I have been on Shore - This Day a Merchant of the City whom I accidentally fell into Conversation with, up the Quay, invited me to dinner, after which he very condescendingly offered to shew me through the Navy Yard - he insisted upon paying all Expenses - we crossed the River in a Steam Boat, and recrossed it on one propelled by Horses, a Thing which I never heard of in England. He gave me an Account of the state of Trade, which he represented as flat and dull at present but I believe, from his account, that trade is not so bad as it is in England by a great deal - every Working Man is paid - I almost said overpaid, for his Labour - even a woman, who is a good Semptress, will earn five or six dollars per week - that is from 40 to 48 New York Shillings.

The Natives of this country, as far as I know at present, are remarkably good Workman - The Mechanics of almost all descriptions may come over from England to learn - particularly Iron-founders, brass founders, Tinplate workers, engravers, watchmakers, Tailors, Shoemakers, etc. etc. Farming is the best Trade followed even in the Neighborhood of this City, were Land, I am told, lets high - but before I write again, I will get particulars upon the Subject.

Horses are remarkably fine, clean limbed Creatures in this city - I am told there is not a greased horse in the whole State - I have not yet learned the price of Provisions generally, in this Country; suffice it to say, all are good and plentiful - there is a capital Market Place in this City, which is well supplied with everything, every Day in the week; Cherries, Raspberries, Strawberries, Pineapples, Limes, oranges, Lemons, new potatoes, Collyflowers, Peas, Beans, Cabbages, and amany sorts of greens, unknown in England.

So far may be shown to my Friends, to whom I desire my best respects; what follows is only for the Inspection of my Wife and children, and is requested to by cut from this paper by my Son John, and Kept for private use.

Note written along the margin of the first page:
In my next letter (to Brother or Mr. Brettargh) I will send a great deal of Useful Information to Emigrants, in respect to laying in Sea Stores, conduct during the Voyage - performing Quarantine - Season to Sail - recommendation of particular Vessels, landing at New York, conduct of Officers here - what seems best to be paid to the Captain for permit and Hospital Money, etc. etc. Things w'd render Knight's Emigrant's Guide[1] more than Double its present value - I will write, please God, in 10 or 14 days - my Head is muddy; not yet clear of the Sea.

Note written along the margin of the second page:
The Hercules and Albion which sailed the same Day we did from Liverpool made their passage one in 27, the other in 28 Days - we were 53 Days - The (*blank space in the letter*) is not yet arrived - Mr. Brettargh will remember the dirty leaky old vessel - always cheaper. A regular trader tho passage be dearer, it may perhaps be cheaper in the end on account of its shortness - the Hercules is sailed again.

My Dearest and Loving Wife and Children,

I have often had you in Remembrance during my long and tedious passage and many times in the night have I seen my children come prancing towards me, Frances generally outstripped her Sister Hannah to meet me with Eyes like two Diamonds of the purest water with all the freedom which she ought to do. Hannah next with blushing Cheeks, appeared half pleased, and half afraid. Next Maria with the same careless indifference as usual - then Eliza came skipping with her pretty little face much in the same manner as her Sister Frances - James generally after slyly looking at me laid his Belly upon a Chair and threw his Heels up and looked again etc. Such moments were the most pleasing moments I have passed, tho' none of them have been miserable since we parted.

I have kept a Journal of the weather and remarkable incidents which happened during our Voyage - by which I find I was not more than three Days sea sick throughout our Passage - the weather was sometimes boisterous, and the winds generally against us - we had upwards of 60 men, women and Children passengers, - one Family from Montgomeryshire in Wales consisted of a Man his Wife (out of the lunatic assylum) and ten Children, a Dissenting Minister from Ruthvin or near it, his Wife (near her time, now she does not count a fortnight) and three very small and very pretty good Children - another Farmer from Wales his Wife and four Children - this man would eat as much at one meal as any four Persons on Board - he got nicknamed the "old Trencher Man" - two others from Wales with Wives and two Children each, one of whom an active man I paid three Dollars to cook, wash linen, clean shoes etc. for me during our passage - several single women from Wales coming over to seek service - one married woman running away from her Husband and Child about 2 years old to seek a Shelter in the western State - several young men from Wales - two Families from Yorkshire - one from the City, and the other from Keighley, his name is Oldridge, has been a distiller of mint and a Barber and Schoolmaster - a number of young men radical Reformers from Huddersfield - old Thomas Leigh and son Thomas from Worsley - a man from (*unreadable*) - Several from Scotland etc. etc. - composed our company.

I generally retired to Bed at eight and arose about 5 in the morning - eat no suppers - When we arrived our Provisions were all done or nearly so - a many had not a meal left and few for more than two Days - I sold Bread to 4 Persons out of my stock and Butter twice. The Ships Crew was upon short allowance for about 15 Days before we arrived - we had very cold Weather during the whole of our journey - much colder than it is in England - in general we were very peaceable.

Dear Wife I often think of your trying and difficult situation - but I hope and trust in God you will get well out of Bed again - be sure not to listen to false tales nor let them disturb you - be cautious with you open your mind when oppressed - do not do it to any but our Son John or his Uncle William who I am certain will keep it a Secret and give you good advice - do not I most earnestly entreat you give way to grief - nor Scold the Children when they do wrong - remember that much scolding makes them careless and naughty- But I hope and am sure they will be good - for that which I hear a bad report of I will bring no Presents, no not anything when I return, but a whip for Correction. Give my dear Girls and little James, each a loving kiss in my name, and say I sent it them together with my Blessing and prayers to God for their Health and Happiness - to my Son John I send a Father's Blessing and Kindest Respects - I hope, nay I believe, I need not request him to be sober and diligent, kind and attentive, to his Mother and Sisters and all Persons, not to be too communicative, but keep his own and his Master's Secrets, and endeavour to the utmost of his Power to acquire the Knowledge of his Profession and serve his Master faithfully and diligently - to whom I desire him to give my best respects, and to his Son Thomas, hoping that John and him will live in friendship together and endeavour to leave off childish pets and whims.[2]

To my Dear Mother and Brothers and Sisters, I send my best and kindest Respects, and to all my Friends - and I will write to them in rotation, hoping they will shew each other my Letters, which shall give them every Information it is in my power to acquire relative to this astonishing Country - As yet, I have seen nothing of it -

Tomorrow I am going to see Mr. Cobbett Jr. he lives about 3 mile from N. York on Long Island - my present Clothing is quite too warm, tomorrow I shall be clothed in the Summer Dress of this Country -

Dear Wife I can scarcely refrain from scribbling on but my Paper is finished, believe me to be in Heart and Mind your Loving husband

James Stott

Note written along the margin of the third page
To every Friend who inquires after me say I send my best respects - I cannot I have not room to name them all - I shall direct this to Son John hoping his Master will give him time to walk up to Pendleton to read it for his mother and Sister - and tell Frances she should learn to keep a Secret and then teach her Sisters - not tell her Schoolmates all she hears said - I shall write again when I leave this City for Philadelphia in about 8 or 10 Days - and then I will tell you how to direct for me - as yet I do not know - Saturday morning the 26th very hot.

Letter addressed to:
Mr. Jn. Stott, at Mr. F Goadsby's, Chymist, Chapel Street, Salford,
Manchester

[1]*Knight's Emigrant's Guide was written by John Knight and printed by M. Wilson in Manchester, England in 1818. It contained information concerning the United States including climate, "manners and disposition of its inhabitants," prices of land, taxes, wages of labour, arts, manufacturing, and English laws on emigration.*

[2]*James' son John was serving an apprenticeship with a chemist and druggist in Manchester.*

Philadelphia in the Early Nineteenth Century

For its role in the birth of the United States, Philadelphia became synonymous with freedom and liberty. Boasting a population of 112,772 in 1820 (Rosenwaike 16), it led the nation in manufacturing. In addition to the many small industries, Philadelphia was a center for the production of lumber, iron, woolen and cotton goods, glass, earthen and stone ware, steam engines, and ships. Known as a cultural and educational center, the Philadelphia Library was founded in 1731 by Benjamin Franklin and by 1830 its holdings exceeded 24,000 volumes. The Academy of Natural Sciences was established in 1817; the Philadelphia Museum had been in operation since 1784; and the Franklin Institute was established in 1804 for the encouragement of manufacturing and the mechanical arts. The University of Pennsylvania was charted in 1779, and the city also boasted a Medical College and College of Pharmacy. The Law Academy was started in 1821, the year after James' arrival (Gordon [a] 349-369).

The infrastructure of Philadelphia was maintained partially by a tax on real and personal property. All major roads leading into and out of Philadelphia had been paved (with broken stone) by 1820. The city had constructed four reservoirs, several botanical gardens, and three prisons. Public schools had been instituted for instruction of the poor, and the Pennsylvania Hospital had been operational since 1750. Numerous social agencies, such as the Society for the Abolition of Slavery and a home for single, indigent women, were working to improve the lives of those needing assistance (Gordon [a] 349-369). This then was the city that James chose as his next destination.

Arrival in Philadelphia

In the letter James wrote to Hannah between July 19 and July 27, 1820, he included a few facts about the conditions in Philadelphia, e.g. the price of land, and items of news concerning other English immigrants. For the most part, however, this correspondence concentrated on James' worry about the welfare of Hannah and their children. As there had not been sufficient time for him to receive mail from England, James still possessed no information about the outcome of the birthing. That he was feeling very far removed from his family is obvious.

James did mention that the "trade is very dull here," which can be documented. The first serious financial setback occurred following the end of the War of 1812. Domestic woolen and cotton manufacturers were struggling to stay in business. Prices dropped sharply, many banks experienced failure, and properties were being foreclosed. Protective tariffs enacted in 1816 prevented further damage to the economy (Lankevich 61), but as James commented, immigrants from England "are not doing so well in general, as they are represented to be doing in Letters" sent home.

LETTER THREE

Philadelphia July 19 to 27. 1820

My dearest Wife/

I have a thousand Questions to ask, but am grieved to think it will be so long before I can receive an Answer; and I have a thousand Things to tell you, that I have seen, and which have befallen me since we parted; but am afraid I shall forget one half of them; one Idea banishes another, they become confused, and I shall surely have omitted the most interesting matter when my letter is concluded. Well, I cannot help it; my Heart affects my Head, and my hand trembles while I write to you - I hope you have before this safely got your Bed, and are doing well; I need not advise you to take care of the little one; Boy or Girl, it will be welcome to me. Many a time have I seen you within these 20 days back, but when I awoke "behold it was all a dream."

I hope our dear Children are all well, and endeavor to comfort their Mother - John I am sure will do all he can to make you comfortable. Hannah will nurse you and little baby, and do all she can to keep the House clean and clothes mended - she knows better than to play with bad girls and learn their wicked Habits - Frances will assist her Sister Hannah in the House and mind her work at School; she knows much better than to be pert and saucy, particularly now that I am in America - I will bring her nothing Home if she be not good, I am sure she would admire to see the little girls here dressed in the Summer fashions, in India Silks and muslin's and French Lace, silk stockings, and such Handsome reticules[1] - they are dressed much finer here every Day, than the Children are dressed at Manchester on Sunday - but about 30 of them died last week in consequence of eating fruit which was not fully ripe - they had been told not to eat it, - when Children act contrary to the wishes and desires of their Parents, they must abide the Consequences; I would wish Frances to read this, and seriously consider of it.

Maria I hope has given over pulling her Face, and shrugging up her shoulders as she used to do; she is now old enough to mind her Book, and endeavour to improve in useful learning; if she be not good and kind, let me know when I return and I will reward her accordingly. Eliza, and what shall I say to the little Chatter-box; why I hope she has minded her Book and that she can now read writing; and that she has not forgot the many little poems she could have said when I left her; but that she pleases and amuses her mother, and her uncle with saying new ones which she had learned since - she surely is a very good girl; for she knows better than to be naughty; I hope she gives her mother no occasion to scold her for dirtying her frock or for doing anything else that is wrong. James is strutting in trousers now; how I see him running across the room laughing at me, laying his belly upon a chair and throwing up his Heels, he appears as hearty as Buck - how I love to dwell upon these things; there is nothing pleases me so well, as holding fancied conversations with my Wife and my Children.

You may tell Mrs. Hamilton that Catherine Walker is married to John Sidebotham; that she is near her Time, and that her husband is gone into the western Country, and that he went the Day after they were married; which I understand from another source is about three months since - I am informed (though Mrs. Walker's family don't speak upon the subject), that John has been a great expense to the old man - he was a partner in the spirit trade - but that was but for a short period - he is an assistant in a store I understand at present, about one thousand miles from here.

Mrs. Ramsden the wife of James Ramsden, from the Jolly Butcher, Little Park, Middleton, arrived here about 14

Days back. She has four children, the oldest about seven years; her Husband was gone into the western states, some time before she arrived - she knows not where he is - poor woman she knows not what to do - she is very disconsolate, and needy without money - I have started a subscription for her, and left papers at different Taverns frequented by Englishmen, soliciting relief for her - there is now about 10 Dollars subscribed, and that will keep her and Children several weeks here. I have seen amany people out of England since I came here and am sorry to say, that Englishmen are Englishmen's worst enemies; they backbite and run each other down.

Trade of every kind is very dull here; and my Countryman are not doing well in general, as they are represented to be doing in Letters which some of them send home. Farming is the best Trade - tell Mr. Knowles that there (*several words missing*) coal anywhere within 100 or 120 miles of either New York or Philadelphia - this is a new Country - it has lately been thrown up from the sea, not above 200 Years since I am sure - Liverpool Coal is as cheap as any in the market and now sells 30 cents per Bushel, one hundred Cents are one Dollar (about a halfpenny each) - when I have found Coal I will write him, and I am now going beyond the Blue Mountains, where it is said to lie in such Quantities - when you get Son John to answer this, give me all the Particulars you can; and he will perhaps get to copy the Letters which I have sent to Messrs. Bancroft, Brettargh, (*unreadable*) and read them to you. Tell Mr. Brettargh a Farmer who came in the ship with me has bought 200 acres about 8 or 10 miles from this City at 15 Dollars per acre - he has about 60 or 70 acres of young thriving wood -worth all the money he gives - the rest is good plow land - he has since had 1000 Dollars, bidden for his Bargain! He pays 1500 down and 1500 more in 5 years, with Int.

Direct for me at Mr. Walker's 37 Cherry St. North 4th Street Philadelphia - send the Letter by the regular courier ships to New York, the 1st of the month - put them in the Letter Bag at the Merchant's Coffee House Liverpool and three pence with each Letter (I think it is) - be mindful they are put in right. -

Tell Sam Garner's mother at Charles Town her Letter to her son is not yet arrived and that he sailed this morning for Canada (Montreal) with Bennett- from then they will come to England, I believe as soon as they can - he told me to say she need not write again till she hears from him.

Kiss my children for me and tell them how I love them - but dearest wife it is impossible to tell how well I love you, and to express the affection of your loving Husband.

James Stott. July 24, 1820

Dear Son John, I have only room to request you will take this letter up to your Mother as soon as your Master can spare you, to whom be pleased to give my best respects - always be obedient and kind and civil to him - tell him I have seen Thomas Seddon of Ringley and his Daughter, they were at the New Jerusalem Meeting House in South 12th Street on Sunday last - I had not much discourse with him - the Rev. Mr. Carle is minister - he cannot explain the Word and show the meaning in so lucid and plain a manner as Mr. Hindmarsh - I enquire as I go along for readers of the Baron's writing - hoping you are well I am Dear Son, your affectionate

Father James Stott

Letter addressed to:
John Stott, at
Mr. Goadsby's Chymist etc.
Chapel Street
Salford

Manchester

¹A reticule is a woman's drawstring bag used as a carryall.

Journey to Pittsburgh and Beyond

Somewhat concerned about a rumored yellow fever epidemic in Philadelphia, James decided to travel to Pittsburgh. As a mining engineer, that part of America held a special interest for him. By 1820, Pittsburgh had a population of 7,248. It was a commercial center, its rivers and railroad conduits for trade. The presence of coal, iron foundries, and mills (glass, cotton, woolen, and paper), had given the city much celebrity. Factories were producing plows, machinery for mills, stoves, steamboats with their engines, and cannon balls, to name but a few of the manufactured items. Most visible to those traveling to Pittsburgh were the large numbers of people and their supplies being readied for embarkation to the western parts of North America (Gordon [a] 378-379).

In August, James directed his fourth letter back to England to his son John. His description of Pittsburgh and its inhabitants was somewhat dismissive, characterizing the city as dirty and coal blackened and the people less than friendly. In short order, James headed to the surrounding territory, traveling as far as Wheeling and Steubenville. Upon his return, he provided much detail about the Pittsburgh "back country," including land cost, produce prices, construction of homes, and the quality of life.

LETTER FOUR

Pittsburgh Aug. 16th 1820

Dear Son/
I started from the fine City of Philadelphia on the morning of Tuesday the 1st. (*unreadable*) it having been rumoured for some Days back that the yellow fever was in the Town, but of this there was no certain proof before the Public; now the board of Health, established to report Fever and as much as possible to prevent the contagion from spreading, daily publish their Bulletins by which it appears that on some Days 2 cases are reported to them, in some Days none, but in no instance more than 4 during the week ending the 10th. Instant it appears there had been 127 Deaths in the City of which 12 were reported, to have died of Malignant Fever - they do not all die that are seized with this Mortal Disease.

The weather is exceedingly hot at present, and the nights are almost as hot as the Days, which tends to make it still more uncomfortable to me - this Town is situated on a flat Bottom of Land between the two fine rivers Monongahela and the Allegheny, which at present are very low, the former is a dull dead stream, the latter is a fine brisk pellucid River. There is lately built, over each River, a new wood Bridge; that over the Monongahela has Seven arches, each 66 yds. span, besides the thickness of the Piers[1] - it cost 130 thousand Dollars to build it - that over the Allegany (it is spelled two ways) has 6 arches of the same size.

The city (for so it is called) is stiled by the inhabitants the Birmingham of America, on account of Trade - but alas! The sound of the hammer is scarcely heard within it; and the hum of cotton or woollen machinery was never heard. It has a dark, a black appearance owing to coal being chiefly burned within it.

Here are amany English people; some from Manchester, one from near your Grandmother's of the name of Winders; several from W. Oldham; one from the Top of Heap near Heywood, and several out of Yorkshire, from near Halifax and Huddersfield - but generally speaking they wish themselves at home again - they do not take part with each other as they ought to do - they quarrel and run each other down - the Irish bear the sway here, the City being chiefly composed o persons from that country - they sometimes squabble, but in general they stick well together - the Town contains from 5 to 6 Thousand People.

The Rivers before mentioned unite at the bottom of the Town and are then called the Ohio River where formerly stood Fort du-quesne, when this place was in possession of the French.[2] The Fortifications were erected here, on purpose to protect the upper Countries from the predatory excursions of the Red Men, who were accustomed to ascend the Rivers, in their Canoes for hundreds of miles - it is only about thirty years since they left the neighborhood - both Banks of these Rivers are very high, rugged and rocky, and the land in general poor. Go up the Allegheny about 15 to 20 miles and you will meet with some pretty good Bottoms; (so the low land, on the Banks of Rivers, in this Country is generally called) and Banks regularly sloping; all covered with large Trees, and thick underwood; here you might easily get a waggon load of Filbert Nuts in one Day, they are so plentiful: it is the only place in America where I have seen the Hazle grow.

The land near "Logan's Ferry" (the place I am now writing about) is chiefly good, and was sold last winter, at Philadelphia by public Auction, it being then the property of a Bankrupt; one Plantation I have visited was purchased by a Mr. Blakeley from near Saint Helen's or Prescot - it is a fine Farm, of 212 Acres, old measure, perhaps it may be

250 Acres; for the old measures were taken when Red
Men had possession of the Country; and who were apt to
shoot the Surveyors as they run along the woods; which
made them not be to particular, only minding to place the
notches upon the Trees, so as to let the owner have measure
enough. Mr. Blakeley has about 60 Acres of clear land
(the rest being covered with wood), an old log House and
Barn in bad condition; for all of which he gave rather less
than five dollars per acre. The Great Road to the River
from the back Country goes through his woods; though
called the Great Road, you can but just perceive the Track
of footsteps which have bended down the grass, it is best
known by the Glade through the wood; as the timber has
been cut down some time or other to form it.

The inhabitants of the Back Country; for so the high
lands, a distance from the River's Banks are called, are
what are here called Squatters; that is persons who have
gone into the Back woods, and squatted themselves down
anywhere they found a plot of ground that suited them -
built themselves an House etc. cleared land to grow them
corn and wheat, got a Horse and a Cow, and live there to
this Day, rearing numerous families, and neither knowing
nor caring who is the real owner of the Plantation they are
squatted upon - In this manner is the Back Country peopled
at this time so near as 16 miles to Pittsburgh.

The next Farm to Mr. Blakeley's, is rented by a man of
the name of Davis, it contains 250 Acres - has about 25
Acres clear, a log House and a falling down Barn for which
he gives 30 Dollars per year! He can keep as many Cows
as he pleases, they run in the woods with Bells around their
necks etc.

Farmer's produce sells very low at present in Pittsburgh,
for cash - but that is very scarce indeed. Wheat at 40 cents
a Bushel to 50 cents; Indian Corn 25 cents; Oats 12 and
one half cents; Beef 4 to 6 cents per lb. Butter 10 to 12 and

one half cents - Mutton is not good, it sells by the joint or Quarter - you may buy a decent Sheep for a Dollar - A Cow and Calf for 10 to 12 Dollars - a decent Waggon and four horses, I saw sold by the Sherriff for Taxes for 130 Dollars. The Horses went at 17 and one half Dollars each, and the waggon 60 Dollars - I noticed the measures are much smaller here than in England - their Corn Measure is no more than our Wine Measure - milk Measure the Same - a Bushel of potatoes only weighs from 60 to 62 lbs. - they are very ordinary, but they sell the dearest of any produce raised - An English Farmer might do very well on the Seaboard by ra(*words missing*) and potatoes.

In this Country are few Brick or Stone Houses, they (*words missing*) Log or Frame Houses - some of the log Houses, which are build of (*word missing*) Timber are miserable looking Huts. - In short the Western Country (*word missing*) a Sort of wilderness - in some places the people are 10, in some 15, (*word missing*) are even as much as 30 miles from a place of worship (*word missing*) die they are buried in their own Lands - whether any funeral (*word missing*) is performed over them, I cannot say.

At the town of Wheeling (*word missing*) Burial Ground lies open to the Hogs and Dogs, and those ami(*rest of word and start of next word missing*)niverous, are constantly in Search of prey -

Ugly as the above Sketch looks (*sketch not reproducible*), a rough Log House looks ten times worse -

When I arrive in England you will have may more (*unreadable*) a many Sketches I have taken of the Shalas Mountains - Towns - Rocks - Bridges etc etc etc.

Since a part of the above I have been at Wheeling, Steubenville etc down the Ohio River - but on account of the Sickness down the River I returned sooner than I should have done - I heard of Riding through Forests guided by notches on Trees, directing by a Pocket Compass etc etc -

but I did not go so far -

Give my kind love to your Mother and Brother and Sisters - to your Uncles, Aunts, etc, to Mr. Goadsby and to all enquiring Friends - your Uncle William will supply you with Pocket Money - I am dear Son your Affectionate Father

James Stott

Sept 8. 1820

P.S. I will write to your Mother in the Course of a few Days I intend to return by way of Washington & Baltimore and shall perhaps see Mrs. Corbett. I have bought a Horse to ride over the Mountains. Shall start in few Days.

Note written along the margin of the third page:
Call upon Mr. Bancroft and give my best Respects - I wrote to him and J. Brettargh from Wheeling - by the same post as this, I write to your Uncle William

Letter addressed to:
Mr. John Stott at Mr. Goadsby's, Chymist Druggist, Salford, Manchester.

By the Amity to Liverpool

[1]*In the margin next to this sentence this multiplication appears:*
yds
66
7
462
38
500

[2]*The area that encompasses Pittsburgh, originally the site of Indian villages, was claimed by the French in 1754 when they erected Fort Du Quesne. The fort was abandoned to the British*

in 1758 and renamed Fort Pitt. The city itself was founded in 1765 and surveyed for lots and farms in 1784. (Gordon [a] 379).

Return to Philadelphia

Four months had passed since James' arrival in America. Clearly, he expected to have mail from England awaiting him upon his return to Philadelphia. Finding no letters at all, James expressed alarm in his correspondence dated October 31, 1820. His tone echoed "great uneasiness" about what might have befallen his wife, his newborn child, his family, and friends. Considering the circumstances of James' departure and his uncertainty about the actions his "enemies" might take, his anxiety must have been great.

Although James did share some of what he was learning about life in Philadelphia, the focus of his attention was still obviously on England and on his immediate course of action. His thoughts fluctuated between outright fear and hurt, finding it difficult to believe that no one had bothered to answer any of his lengthy messages. All of James' previous letters had been carefully and beautifully written. This following communication was, at times, fragmented with words apparently omitted. He attempted to discuss his recent observations and relay newsworthy encounters, but questions laced with dread concerning his family filled the greater portion of his four page plea for some word that the Stotts were safe and well.

LETTER FIVE

Philadelphia Oct. 31st 1820

Dear Wife/

For so by the established formality of writing, I must still call you, and so in truth you really are dear and very dear - for many a feeling Pang have you caused me within these few Weeks back. Know that I have written amany Letters to you, and Son John, Brother William, to my Mother I have sent two, and more and more to my Friends - but all my writing is of no avail - I cannot receive, I have not received an answer. I often say, my Friends, my Brother, my Son (may not my son) may forsake me, but my Mother and my Wife, my dear Wife, they never will. They never can forsake me. They will remember that such a Being is that once was dear to them. Then I say my Brother William, and my Friends would write to me; I am sure - I am certain they would write - nay I am verily persuaded they have written to me - and after musing and weighing the pros and cons I conclude, my enemies have been playing me some foul play.

a ship is arrived in new york which left Liverpool and the Instant (name the White Oak) but she has brought no letter for me. I have heard of the arrival of a many Vessels at Boston, New York, and Baltimore, I have frequently called at our Post office here, after such arrivals but no Letters for me! Several vessels have arrived in this port from Liverpool within these few Weeks; I eagerly enquired of the Captain if he brought any Letter for your Husband, but each of them answered no, no.

I often repeat these few lines out of Goldsmith's Hermit
(Here James quotes eight lines penned by Oliver Goldsmith alluding to the fact that love can feel very

empty, indeed).
to my Wife I would further say with the same poet

(James adapts four lines from Oliver Goldsmith's "The Traveller" in which Goldsmith referred to the idea that travel without the person one loves is often a painful experience).

Some of the letters I have written, I have sent by gentlemen returning to England and some of them I have put into Ship Letterbags sailing from this port, and others I have paid postage to new york, and directed them to go by such and such a vessel to Liverpool. Now I will put the Question that all my letters miscarried I think impossible.

You know I should visit my Friend Mr. Walker. You know his son Richard; of course you could get direction how to send to him and by writing to him, you might have formed a reasonable expectation of hearing some thing of me - I know not how you have acted in these things - your own conscience will bear your witness. This I know, your not writing gives me great uneasiness. I wish I had brought you with me and trusted providence with your safe arrival - the wife of a Welsh clergyman who came along with us, was much in the same state I left you and she stood the Voyage very well - you might have done the same tho' we had a long passage of it - we had amany little Boys and Girls on board - they were very happy and cheerful during the whole journey - they skipped and played like young lambs - our little darlings would have done the same -

The weather is remarkably fine and pleasant here at present, and I am told we may expect it to continue so till Christmas - sometimes till the middle of January before winter sets in -

I have been in amany parts of this large Country considering the short time I have been in it - I have travelled more than fifteen hundred miles - beyond the Blue

Mountains I met with many Persons from England - they do not like the Country - they all wish themselves on the Seaboard East of the Huge Chain of Hills - I have been several Times in Jersey States since my return to this fine city, and find amany Farms upon Sale very cheap, within the distance of from three to sixteen miles - long and good buildings in at the Bargain, from 15 to 50 Dollars per acre according to distance from the City, and the owner wanting money - some of them must sell or the Sheriff will sell for them[a] - good land with indifferent Buildings may be purchased from three to fifteen Dollars per acre - the Roads are good, and the country well peopled -

If you and my dear Children were here, I would bid adieu to the Tyrants of old England - I could never forget for my friends and Relations - methinks I see fell discord with human aspect; Bloody Dagger in one hand, and lighted Torch in the other, hastily stalking towards my native Land - may Heaven preserve all that is dear to my Heart - my wife, my Children, my Relatives, and my numerous Friends!

Weaving goes very well here at present - and weavers are wanted; they can earn from 75 cents to 100 per Day - living is very low in comparison to what it is in England - a Yorkshire man and two Sons (young men) who came over in the same vessel I did, tells me, that they three do live, and better than they did in England and find fire, for 2 Dollars per week, that is nine english Shillings - He has sent for his wife and remainder of the Family[b] being well assured he and they can do better here than a man who lives upon 50 acres of his own land can do in England.

If I do not receive letters in the course of 14 days advising me what to do, I will pitch my Tent for the Winter at all events, and begin to do something to earn my Bread - I will continue to write monthly to you untill I receive an Answer - you know that a Vessel sails regularly the first of each month from Liverpool for New York - of course you could surely get some friend to put you a Letter in the Ship's Letter bag on board the Vessel and (*unreadable words*) come from New York to me. I will either send my letters (*unreadable word*) New York (*unreadable words*) of each month or by some Gentleman or other that is returning to Liverpool, Manchester etc - I intend to send this by Mr. Frank Ward of Nottingham who is returning with his Family to England - he has been here 12 months and never offered, that I know of to do anything - his Family do not like it and he is returning on their account.

I yesterday dined with Henry Chorley of Broomhouse lane - he married James Barlow's Daughter of Drywood in Worsley; he lives about a mile and a half from the city, upon a beautiful Farm of 45 acres, he finds all the Labour and half the Stock; and has half the produce - (*unreadable word*) and large kitchen Garden - he keeps thirteen cows and (*unreadable word*) Horses etc - I am sure he will do very well upon it - his Brother Ashton Barlow is Farming for a Gentleman near Wilmington and I am informed is doing very well. I sincerely wish your Sister Lydia and Family were here. I am certain that her Husband and her, with their working Family might live as well as most gentlemen in England, and moreover save money in a few years to purchase them a Farm -write to her with my love and best respects and tell her what I say. I have written to our nephew Richard Tattersall before I went over the Mountains (hard journey) but have received no Answer! As my experience increases I find eight people may live very well here if they are steady and industrious, but I am sorry to say a many of them are not - they love liquor and it is cheap here. I will only write one letter more to my Friends till I have heard from them. give my best respects to them all. I hope my friend N. A Knowles got my two letters safe, giving him a Description and Sketch of the Coal Mines and different Shatas over the Blue Mountains - give my Children each a kiss of comfort from their Father - tell them I am in perfect health, no cough nor spitting, and look ten years younger than when I left them - the air here is very pure and clear - with love and respects to Son John, Brother William and all Relatives. I am my dearest Wife, your loving true and faithful Husband   James Stott

P.S. Since writing the above, I see by the Books at the Merchants Coffee House that the Ship Nestor (Packet) is arrived at New York (yesterday). I called at the post office here but I feel very unhappy now - there is no letter for me! Pray God send you are all as well as you should be - J. S. Nov. 2. 1820

Note written along the margin of the third page
Mr. M. Walker and his family are all in good Health - his School increases - they wish to be kindly remembered to all friends. Catherine has got a little daughter which she calls Sarah - her Husband is down the Ohio river, about 900 miles from here.

Note written along the right margin of the fourth page
James Stott's respectful compliments to Mr. Goadsby - will thank him to let his Son John take this letter up to his Mother the very first opportunity - P.S. Mr. Ward will not pass through Manchester

Note written across the bottom of the fourth page
I have lately sent a letter by a Mr. Cardwell to Mr. Bancroft - he promised to deliver it himself. Mr. Cardwell has been here sometime selling goods for different Houses (his Brother & C. have a warehouse in (Cannon Street) Manchester - if Mr. B has not rec'd it tell him to look after it - I think I omitted to mention in it that if any of my Friends be coming here would do well to bring woollen yarn & worsted. It sells high here - Yeald yarn too would pay well, there is no manufacture of it in the United States - weavers in general have Cotton Yealds - Copper Vessels, needles, pins, plates, China etc are sold very high here - write to my Brother Thomas - give him my best

respects - tell him I take it hard he does not answer my letters - he could easily put a letter into the bags of any vessel that is sailing to Boston, Providence, New York, Philadelphia, Baltimore etc etc. - any by paying a few pence with it - it would be sure to come. - I am determined not to return till I hear from you - please to give Mr. Walker's comp'ts to Mr. Hamilton, & mine too.

Note from the left margin of James' letter referring to his first flagged sentence
[a]during the War when produce sold high, the owners mortgaged their farms for as much they will sell for now - they spent their money, now the Mortgagee wants it in - the Sherriff is applied to - the land is sold low etc etc

Note from the bottom of James' letter referring to his second flagged sentence
[b]Since writing the above I have been over to see him - his Wife etc are just arrived - he only wrote for them when I sent 2nd letters to you and Friends - he has the pleasure of receiving his wife and Family. I cannot have that of a single letter - She was only 22 Days in coming from Liverpool - I am afraid something is wrong.

Letter addressed to:
Mr. John Stott
at Mr. Goadsby's, Chymist & Druggist
Chapel Street Salford
Manchester *Letter is stamped* "Liverpool Ship Letter"

Chapter III
Stopping over the Winter

A Mail Packet from England

At long last James heard from his family. His relief was palpable and the tone of his sixth letter reflected just that. It was filled with observations about America as well as many references to the problems in his homeland, those references sparked by newspapers and publications included in the mail packet from his son John.

Clearly, James was still focused on conditions in England. He spent much of his text discussing the Reformist newspaper the *Manchester Observer* and the writings by William Hone (1780-1842), publisher and political satirist famous for his pamphlets including *The Political House That Jack Built*, published in 1819. Widely read throughout the country and well known for his cleverly penned radical reform views, Hone was prosecuted and brought to trial three times for his writings; eventually, he was acquitted (Rickword 1-18).

Another radical writer mentioned by James and cited earlier in this book, was Samuel Bamford (1788-1872), who resided in James' childhood hometown of Middleton. Bamford had led the Middleton contingent to the Manchester "Peterloo" meeting and was subsequently arrested for doing so (Read 37). He was serving a one year's sentence in prison to be followed by a monitored five year period of good behavior (Read 153). Although James was somewhat dismissive of Bamford's confinement, the terror felt by Bamford's wife on the night of his arrest and the subsequent reality of being in "lockup" (later described by Bamford in his book, *Passages in the Life of a Radical*, pages 165-179), was probably the very eventuality from which James had fled.

In the remainder of the letter, James made reference to the growing number of revolutions and their effects on sovereigns. Also revealed was the decision he had made regarding his immediate future. Ever the exponent of the use of generalizations, James concluded his remarks with further impressions of Amercians and the quality of life in the United States.

LETTER SIX

Philadelphia Dec 3. 1820

Dear Son/

After rambling to New York for your letter and that from your dear Mother, brought into this country by Mr. F Wrigley, and then back to Philadelphia again, as Mr. W. had started from one place the same hour and Day I started from the other, I at last got them - I assure you my mind had been upon the rack several (many) weeks to hear from you and all my Family and Friends - after writing so many letters and receiving no answer, I began to conclude either that some foul play had been made, in respect to forwarding them, or that something was not well in my Family, your kind and affectionate letters dissipated my unpleasant feelings-

I here thank you for the present of the Newspapers and the two Publications by W. Hone, which you did very well to send me. The Newspapers afford me much Information relative to the State of the Country and to party feelings - I see Manchester Justices are determined to maintain their Character in the Mighty Scale of Evil and Mis-rule - only think of the poor wounded and insulted Radicals at Oldham[1] - I am sincerely glad that you have got such an independent, well got up paper as the *Manchester Observer*, it is now better edited that it ever was since its commencement and I sincerely hope Mr. Evans will conquer his opponents with the Sword of Truth; at all events I hope he will continue to bend his Bow and empty his Quiver at the Tyrants; some random Arrow, "Shot at the venture" will assuredly reach the Heart of Jehoshaphat, and when the Master Evil is removed its attendants will disperse like Chaff before the wind - Solomon says "even the wicked are for the Days of evil," and we know that Storms and tempests purify the air-

In respect to Hone's publications, they are super excellent, I have shown them to some hundreds of Englishmen as well as Americans who all admire them much - when the *Ladder*[2] is explained to an American he laughs loud; the Scene call Cats meat quite tickles their fancy indeed - I think it is one of his best Hits and he has certainly made amany good ones - the leech in the lanthorn is a fine idea; it conveys a double meaning - indeed the whole is excellent - the other work[3] is the most exquisite piece of Satire ever written, it cannot make an English Lord (*words unreadable*) on account of his education, but (*word unreadable*) may (*words unreadable*) feel for him - as for the grandman who stands at the Bar of Justice he can do no wrong - I cannot but remember the Clock being out of order upon amended motion; it is ordered to be marched in yesterday!!!

In the *Manchester Observer* there is a numerous collection of exquisite things. I much admire Bamford's "Song of the Slaughter," and had I not seen his, I would have sent you one which I have written upon the same occasion - poor Bamford! but his 12 months will soon be over and during his confinement he will have Time and Leisure to improve his mind. I hope he has friends now out of Lincloln Castle, with Hearts so generous and purses so sufficiently lined as not to suffer him want

Since beginning to write this letter, I have engaged a Store at 206 South Street, where I intend to spend the winter, and think I can get more Information and Knowledge of the Country then could be gained in walking the Streets during cold months; In my letter to your dear Mother I will add all the Particulars in my power and state my Reasons at length, for concluding to stop the Winter here, - understand that I have only engaged the house for five Months, and can quit it sooner if convenient for me - during the few Days I have been here I cannot say I relish the Business, everything is new and I feel awkward and strange - but practice will render things more pleasant and comfortable I expect

You have heard of the Revolution in the Island of St. Domingo and that it is now wholy Republican; how do you think the great Folks at London will like it, will they acknowledge a Republic; or will they declare War against President Boyer? We live in Strange Times - Revolutions upon Revolutions are the order of the Day - what will be the Effect of the fraternal embrace of Sovereigns, time only can determine - but this we may expect, that they met to plan something or other against the Liberty of their Subjects - People of Europe have now learned that Kings and Queens are but men and women. What will little England do? Will it have the Chains rivited (*unreadable*) fitted upon his legs? Mr. Walker thinks it will and so does Mr. John

Wood, and they are both intelligent Gentlemen

There is lately arrived in this City a Mr. Fipping from Manchester; he says he spent more money at the Grey Mare in (*unreadable*) than would have purchased the place and if we may be allowed to judge him by his actions he certainly speaks the Truth, for he has never been Sober since he came ashore - he runs down this Country and its Institutions and intends sailing back this winter; it is such fellows as this that furnish the Editor of the Courier with his flimsy Remarks upon this Country - I allow it is not all that I could wish - but I prefer it to old England as it is at the present governed. This place will never rival it in manufactures - the Children here are too independent, They will only work just as long, and as much as they please - they are all slim made, very smart and active but very impudent - I do not like their manners - they smoke cegars and swear

You asked by about Druggists etc here - I assure you thay are very numerous and each poor Son of the Pestal dubs himself Doctor. There are some hundreds of them in this City - and in respect to Justices and Squires and Attorneys at Law, they are as plentiful as Beggars were at Manchester before Joey and his Gang were employed to take them up - Weaving, Spinning etc goes well at present The poor live much better in this Country than persons of Fortune do with you - a fat Goose is 18 pence to (*unreadable*) shillings, a couple of Rabbits 6 pence 3 farthings - Beef 4 Cents to 6 Cents per pound - Mutton 2 to 4 Cents - Flour 4 Dollars or 18 shillings per Barrel of 196 lbs - Salt Butter 8 pence, new Butter 11 pence per lb. - Cheese 4 and a half pence to 5 pence per lb. - a weaver can and does earn from 6 to 10 Dollars or from 27 shillings to (*unreadable*) per week. House Rents are high - Taxes are low - a Farmer who holds a good House and 200 acres of land only pays 12 Dollars or 54 shillings per year State

Taxes. (*Unreadable*) etc only about 3 pence per acre! Land Rents from 4/6 to 30 shillings per acre according to Distance from the City, Quality, etc - I wish your Aunt Lidia and Family were here - they would do well as both the Cotton and woolen trade goes well - tell Mr. Bancroft Mr. Wood has rec'd the lathe he sent him and is mighty proud of it.

I have scrubbed this over in a very hasty manner so that I have scarcely room left to mention your Dear Mother and Brothers and Sisters - I am proud of little Joseph - your Mother will hear from me perhaps before you read this which will come by the Nestor from New york - be sure to write to me every month by the New york packet which sails from Liverpool on the 1st and let me have the News of the Day - My Heart Aches when I think of you all - be sure to improve yourself as much as you can, and pay the utmost attention to your Business - keep good company and love your Mother and Brothers and Sisters etc. We have had some cold Days - the weather is now delightful - Adieu my son -- God bless you - God bless you

Dec 9th 1820

I shall write to your uncle William by the Ship Rebecca Sims which Sails in a few Days for Liverpool.

Letter adressed to:
Mr. John Stott
at Mr. Goadsby's Chymist & Druggist
Chapel Street
Salford
Manchester Single Sheet

[1] *Oldham was the site of one of the mass protest meetings attended by thousands (Halevy 58).*

[2]*The Ladder referred to by James is a William Hone satirical*

pamplet entitled "The Queen's Matrimonial Ladder" published in London in 1820 (Rickword 167-185).

[3]*The "other work" James discussed is a Hone satire entitled "Non Mi Ricordo!" published in London in 1820 (Rickword 193-208).*

Of Scandal, Sugar Prices, Coinage, and Liberty

James' thoughts were never far from the political climate and his own business affairs in England. As to the latter, a problem with rent collection from his tenants in an apartment building was of great concern to him. He stated that he was "assured that some meddling person" with an ulterior motive was involved in the payment dispute.

Judging from the amount of space used in discussing prices of goods in the United States, his feelings about the people, and the overall living conditions, James was becoming increasingly involved in the workings of the land of his exile. Although James had begun to use the pronoun "we" rather than "they" when referring to Americans and spoke of England as "your" country, he continued to call England "home." The timing of his return, however, appeared to be less and less definite.

It was during this period that the people in the United States were avidly reading about the royal scandal rocking the United Kingdom. In a margin note, James alluded to the Bill of Pains and Penalties against the wife of George IV. He commented on the interest being generated in the escalating royal debacle involving George IV and his determined efforts to divorce his wife, Caroline. Refusing an offer of 50,000 Pounds in exchange for agreeing to remain permanently away from England and renouncing forever her title of Queen upon George's coronation, Caroline returned to the United Kingdom in June of 1820 after six years abroad.

The Bill of Pains and Penalties was the instrument introduced into the House of Lords dissolving the marriage and stripping Caroline of her royal title. A trial in the House of Lords began in August. Public opinion in support of her ran high and crowds gathered as the press reported all of the details. Caroline was accused of adultery and "bedchamber gossip" was widespread (Halevy 89-96). The lengthy trial caused tremendous disruption throughout the country (Trevelyan 192). Finally, in November the bill passed the House of Lords by only nine votes, making it virtually impossible to move it to the House of Commons. Although that action brought the trail to an end (Halevy 98), George continued his opposition to to his wife. Caroline, however, was not one to easily relinquish her royal position. In July of 1821, the coronation was finally scheduled and Caroline, accompanied by her supporters, went uninvited to the ceremony to demand her rightful place. She was turned away at the door. The saga came to an abrupt conclusion when a month later, following a short illness, Caroline died (Halevy 102-103).

An impassioned paragraph expressing James' views on liberty was included in this next letter to his wife. Interestingly, he requested that it go to Mr. Evans (at the *Manchester Observer*), but be printed without revealing the fact that he was the author. One must again conclude that James continued to fear the ramifications of his reformist stand. It is in that paragraph that he also hinted at the possibility of sending for his family and remaining permanently in America.

LETTER SEVEN

Philadelphia Dec 10, 1820

My Dear Wife & Children/
I received the letter which you sent by Mr. F. Wrigley just 29 Days since - my feelings had been tortured for some Time before - my Dearest Wife you certainly should have written sooner - You well knew I should be extremely anxious to hear from you.

In respect to the unpleasant part of your letter I was forewarned of it in a Dream while on Ship board and therefore longed to hear the Particulars because I saw that the whole was not disclosed to me - In respect to the Tenants at Charles Town I am rather surprised at their Behaviour, they have each of them a small Book with receipts in for all the money they paid me, and of course the Books should be shown by them before they say anything to disparage my character - old Mrs. Gardner, can testify they have Books and I am certain she will willingly produce hers because she owes me nothing. The Tenants have all Books and let them be demanded from them - I hope Brother William will not part with any of my accounts to the other Exors. They cannot know he has them except he tells them - he must be sure to keep all the accounts or else how can I set Things in the proper light at my return. I feel assured that some meddling person has been baducing me to Mr. Bradshaw, but from what I felt when I received my Assurance, I believe Brother William will meet with no uneasiness through it.

My Son John writ me a very pretty letter for you, and I thank him kindly for it - I sent to him (yesterday) a letter by the Ship Nestor from N. York - this I intend to convey by the Rebecca Sims, from this port to Liverpool - which will come first to hand. I cannot say, but wish them both a speedy passage and that they may find you all well. In respect to the Contents of your Letter and Information from my much respected Friends, I concluded to stop all Winter; then I shall know both Summer and Winter in America - the weather here is remarkably fine and clear at present, and I am in very good Health, no Cough or Spitting such as used to trouble me in the foggy atmosphere of Lancashire.

Tell my very worthy and much respected Friends J. Brettargh and J. Bancroft that I have looked out for places for them, and have got a great variety. Farms from 40 to 300 Acres each, which may be bought very low for Cash; but Things are now going pretty well here and land has been advancing for this month back.

I have a most pleasant Farm in view of 60 acres of good land and Timber, about 9 miles from the City, and decent Buildings upon it - and upon a good Road, and in a respectable neighborhood, near to four Meeting Houses of different Denominations. The price asked is 2500$ but I dare say 2000 would buy it - 2000$ is 450 pounds sterling. I have taken a Store and Stock in Trade at a Valuation and paid about 300$ for it. I expect it will maintain me (*words unreadable*) this Winter and in the Spring I can easily sell out, as it is situate in a good neighborhood and well established. We cook our victuals, wash up Dishes, etc. ourselves; but I cannot say I like doing so - he is a single man and I observe to him, "we will bring no scandal upon the House by bringing a woman into it." We sell cheese 9 Cents per pound, Butter (Salt) 14 Cents, Flour, superfine, 3 Cents, Ham 12 1/2 Cents, Salt 3 Cents per pint, Coffee 30 Cents per pound, Tea 6 Cents per Oz., fine young Hyson we give 85 Cents per pound for it - Ale is 8 Cents per Quart, Cider 4 Cents per Quart - Wine, red port, 45 Cents per Quart, Brandy the Same (the best French), Brown Sugar 8 to 12 1/2 per pound. Sump Sugar 17 Cents per pound -

New England Rum we sell 18 Cents per Quart, Jamaica Rum 50 Cents per Quart, but little called for, Whiskey 10 cents per Quart, Apple Brandy 15 Cents per Quart - Cordials are about 20 Cents per Quart. Old Bottled Porter 12 1/2 cents per Bottle. Flour is now 4 1/4 to 4.40$ per Barrel.

We have a many different Coins in this country belonging to different Nations of different names and Values, so that I am rather at a loss sometimes in giving Change - We have French Crown 110 Cents, the Frank 95 Cents, the Spanish Dollar 100 Cents, the half $ 50 Cents, Quarter $.25 Cents, the Eleven penny Bit 121/2 Cents, and the Five penny Bit is 6 1/4 Cents. Then we have American coins, Eagles and half Eagles are of Gold, but very scarce. I have only seen two since arrived; The Silver Coins are the Dollar, half Dollar and Quarter Dollar which pay for the same as the Spanish pieces of the same Denomination. Besides these we have 10 Cent pieces and five Cent pieces which pay for the name they bear, our Copper Coins are Cents and half Cents.

Cider is $1 1/2 per half Barrel, Beer we pay $6 per Barrell for, Porklings are sold by the side or quarter, at from 40 to 50 Cents per Quarter according to size, weight from 9 to 14 pounds - a good goose sells for 37 1/2 to 50 Cents, a couple of Ducks about 30 to 40 Cents; a young Rooster of 5 to 6 pounds 20 Cents (the Ladies here will not suffer them to be called Cocks); indeed all sorts of Provisions are reasonable except Milk and potatoes - milk is 6 Cents per Quart and potatoes 50 Cents per Bushel of about (*unreadable*) lb.

Apples are uncommon cheap and the Children of the poorest Class live mostly to Dinners upon Apple Pudding and Apple Pie sweetened with molasses. They Breakfast and Sup upon Coffee & Cream and Toast & Butter, and Salt Fish, or Beef Steak, or Fowls. Sheeps Heads are thrown away. The very poorest of the poor will not have them given. Cows Heads are not saleable articles in this plentiful Country.

The longer I am in America the better I like the Country, but the worse I like the natives of it. In their manners they are not pleasing, in their Dealings, they are all but Honest, except you have them fast be a written contract, and here is no occasion for a Boroughmonger's stamp. Indentured, Leases, Bargains etc. are all upon plain paper - Cheating, they call outwitting, and getting a man's property without paying for, they call grand management, hence arises numerous vexations, and expensive lawsuits which frequently ruin one or both of the Parties; I am sorry to observe them pay so little regard to the Sanctity of an Oath. They are much addicted to drinking cheap hot, and fiery Spirits (I mean the lower Classes) which not infrequently leads to most violent passions, and sometimes Terminates in Death. The common Law here is the same as the common Law of England; but their penal laws are not half so severe - here they are particularly careful of preserving human Life - smuggling is scarcely punished at all, and is much practiced chiefly by Europeans. Forging Bank notes will, if strong proof be brought against the accused party, subject him to solitary confinement, and hard labour for 12 months, or if the case be much aggravated or the subject an old offender perhaps the Sentence will be from 2 to 5 years. The mail stages are not guarded here as in the old Country, and frequently robberies take place. The post offices are kept by StoreKeepers, Tailors, Shoemakers etc. in the different small Towns the stage passes through. In this Department great improvements have taken place in the last few years, and amany more in the Contemplation.

The people here might live very happily if their Fathers had taught them Domestic Obedience and Sobriety, but these are Virtues much wanted in the Country - even Boys at School refuse to submit to their Teachers; frequent Lawsuits take place between the latter and the parents of Children because the Master has been provoked to give the refractory Urchins such chastisements the parent ought to have rendered unnecessary at School by eliciting proper Subordination at home. One of Mr. J Walker's Scholars recently told his Master to kiss his a__. Old Joseph instantly dismissed him from School. This was a very bad Boy.

In your answer to this, be sure to give me the best opinion you and my Friends can form upon the State of your Country; whether the Tyrants will fall or whether the People will tamely submit to Slavery? If your opinion is that the System can continue, my mind is to fetch you to this Country for I would rather that my Bones should be laid in a foreign land, in a Land of Liberty, than that they should wear the Chains of oppression in the Land of my forefathers; and after Death be upbraided as a Cowardly wretch by their brave Spirits - would they not point the finger, and say "these our Sons? Nay! We fought, we bled, for Liberty! and have they not suffered the base born, to wrench it from them? They have been meaner than a Spaniard! Let them go to the regions beneath and there be flogged to eternity by Castlereagh!" My warm soul shrinks back at the dreadful thought - what is Life without Liberty? Why is it going a long hard journey in a prison yard; you see the high walls, the Locks, Bolts, & Chains and the terrific Keeper continually shaking his whip of Scorpions with one hand, and his bunch of Dungeon Keys in the other.

Note written in the left margin beside the previous paragraph: Give this paragraph to Mr. Evans as an extract of a letter from America & don't give my name to the Public, but give it the Editor

I often see my Dear Children and their Mother in my Sleep. I awake and find myself alone - my heart always beats towards you - my clothes want mending - my shirts are wearing out; my Neck handkerchiefs are done. Who must make the next for me? I look back and remember who made these I have at present. My Daughters could make them if I were at Home - I see Hannah smile, and wipe her nose, and hear her say "I could do these jobs for him." And Frances looks as bright as Gold and says "So could I." Maria takes little notice, Eliza says "I could make him Handkerchiefs - I have done." James appears a fine Boy, but he wakens his Brother Joseph too often out of sleep. I am (*several words unreadable*) Wife has got a Son to call after her revered Father - I think of Joseph many a Time, I should like to see his little pretty face.

Return my warmest Thanks to our Friend J. Brettargh and tell him I hope to have it my power some way or other to repay his kindness to you; I writ to him by the Tuscarora about three weeks back. I hope he has got the letter before now - do not think I forget J. Bancroft and other Friends - no, no, I do not, I cannot - give my best respects to them all - Your Sisters and Friends and Relations in Yorkshire are often in my thoughts - so are my Dear Mother and Brother and Sisters. I have only written one letter to Mr. Halliwell, which he has not yet answered. Give my respects to him, and tell him to mention me kindly to Mr. Sholes of Stakehill - amany farmers are come hither this Fall, and their purchasing land has caused it to rise in price - I hope Mr. Brettargh will write a small hand and put his lines nearer together, for I love to hear the Country News he gave me - tell him to send me all he can when he writes and as I have never failed to write once a month to him and Mr. Bancroft I hope they will not fail to write monthly to me - if any person be coming over this Winter I should like a Bundle of papers, Pamphlets etc.

I lately sent three Books by a Yorkshireman who was returning to Leeds, directed to Mr. Bancroft (he came by the Tuscarora) - The National calendar will give him much Information - after reading I should like him to let my other Friends see it - do not be deceived by the Contents of the other two - now my Loving Wife and dear Children I beg leave to conclude with prayers to Heaven for you to enjoy Health

Yours Affectionately - James Stott.

P.S. get John to write to his Aunt Lidia, I have forget her Husband's name or I would have written to him.

Note written along the bottom margin of the last page:
Take the following from this morning's United States Gazette - "Hard Times in the Missouri and dull Sale for Negroes" - on the 9th of November at Saint Louis, two common looking Negro Men were sold at public auction - one of them was knocked off at 7 Dollars and 11 Cents, and the other at 6 D. and 30 Cents." - Mark, this is the next State to that called Illinois where Mr. E. Grundy is determined to travel to. He would do well to go there, but much better in coming back again - a rumor is afloat this morning (Monday) that the Lords has dismissed the Bill of Pains and Penalties against the Queen - the People of this City appear to take a great Interest in the Trial. It is the leading article in all the Newspapers - we are now waiting very anxiously for the arrival of the New York Packet which left Liverpool the first of November.

(Dec. 11 1820) we have had some Gales upon these coasts during the last three weeks.

Letter addressed to:
Mr. John Stott at Mr. Goadsby's, Chymist & Druggist, Chapel Street, Salford, Manchester

On the Consequences of Passion, Love, Marriage and the Lack of Communication

The eighth letter from James is divided into two sections—one addressed to son John and one to his wife Hannah. In the first we learn a bit more about James' life in America. The majority of the correspondence, however, is devoted to advice to John concerning the pitfalls facing young men as they mature and begin to spend time with young women. His love for Hannah and his children was professed in the second section, followed by an indication that emigration for his family was, in his estimation, becoming a viable option. James' distress at having received very little in the way of communication from his family was again expressed.

Clearly, James had spent many more months away from England than he had originally anticipated. Whether that alone accounted for the lack of response from Hannah, we are unable to discern. Reformer William Cobbett had returned to England from his temporary exile, having stated in his published journal, *A Year's Residence in the United States of America*, "I myself am bound to England for life. My notions of allegiance to country; my great and anxious desire to assist in the restoration of her freedom and happiness; my opinion that I possess, in some small degree, at any rate, the power to render such assistance; and above all other considerations, my unchangeable attachment to the people of England, and especially those who have so bravely struggled for our rights: these bind me to England" (Cobbett 18). Could Hannah have felt that James, with a wife and children in England, held similar views and would be setting sail for Liverpool before another ship mail packet could reach him in Philadelphia? Was Hannah harboring some resentment about his departure and continued absence? Were letters lost in transit? Whatever the explanation for the silences on the part of his family, James was dismayed.

LETTER EIGHT

Philadelphia January 8. 1821.

Dear Son/

As I have made a point of writing to you, your Dear
Mother or to one or more Friends, each month so I take
the opportunity of the Packet Ship James Monroe which
sails from New York the 10th to convey a few lines to you
again; The same conveyance will bring a letter to Messrs.
Brettargh and Bancroft; I wish you all, the best Compliments
of the Season - I have presented my respects to amany
Friends by name in my epistle above alluded to, but have
omitted Mr. E Grundy as I intended to write to him by the
same Conveyance, buy am afraid now, that I shall not have
time, so beg you will desire Mr. Bancroft to present best
Respects and give this as a reason for the omission of his
name.

The winter is set in, I am told, the severest, it has done
these many years back, but in England we should not think
it over cold - In the new England States it appears by the
Newspapers the weather is very severe, but you will always
do well, if you make great allowances for Statements made
in Newspapers - particularly those edited by the Fools of
Despots.

The men of New England are called Yankees , and I
heard an Irishman give a Definition of them the other
evening to the following effect -"You must understand, by
dear Sir, that the Yankees are great Travellers - none of
them, d'ye see, are thought fit to send from Home, until
they can cheat their own Father; then they are dismissed
with a Blessing."

My Dear Son, I hope you will never learn to cheat, hold
out as you have begun - continue to be industrious - use

economy, and meddle not with matters that do not concern you - be more than cautious in trusting your secrets, even to your best Friends; interfere not in domestic Quarrels - live Soberly - avoid wanton Company of both Sexes - I cannot caution you, in regard to fixing your Affections further than this, be sure to keep the best genteelist, and most virtuous Company you can - and then if your young Heart goes, it goes to one the most amiable and virtuous you have been able to introduce yourself to - let not your passions entice you, Remember the old adage "that the Passions are good Servants, but bad, very mad Masters." Therefore, bite your Lip, lay your Hand upon your Breast, and by every other Means, endeavour to keep them under. When you feel great agitation in your Breast, besure to hold your Tongue - there is nothing which young men, in general, want more, then Sense to hold their Tongues at certain Times - whenever the Heart is exhilarated the Tongue would needs wag; and that is the Time when they ought to be most cautious in speaking, or most careful of their Words.

My Dear Son, there are certain evil private practices - I dare say, nay I hope, you have not learned them - I conjure you never do - I was married to your Mother before I knew such evils existed - I hope John Stott, will never commit an Act in private which his Heart would be ashamed of the world knowing - and I further hope he will preserve a heart susceptible of the most delicate and chaste Feelings. Never trust a Secret to a boon Companion - never believe a Man the sooner, for swearing all he says is true.

For the next four years, you ought to be particularly careful of your Health - in order to preserve it, be sure to keep good honest Hours. Endeavour to the utmost of your power, to obtain and preserve the good word, and good opinion of your Master during the Term of your apprenticeship; it will be a passport to Prosperity when your Term is expired, and be the greatest promoter of ease & comfort during the time you have to serve.

Love your Dear Mother and Brothers and Sisters, and all your relatives and friends each in his proper Circle, according to Mr. Pope's Simile - and endeavour to comfort them under their several afflictions - I have been rather negligent in some of these Duties, tho not in all of them - Love God above all Things, and endeavour to worship him in spirit and in Truth - return not evil for evil, "But do unto others as you would that others should do unto you"- The above, my Dear Son, is the best Christmas Box which I can throw you across the Atlantic, by the Ship James Monroe from New York - I conjure you keep the precepts above contained, as you would the apple of your Eye - read them frequently, and practice them oftener.

I shall preserve the remainder of this sheet for to convey a few lines to your Mother and Sisters at Pendleton. I think it very strange that I cannot hear from you oftener - only one poor Solitary Letter in 8 months, - remember how often you have heard from me either directly, or by Friends - consider the pain caused by suspense - be more punctual through life with correspondents than you have been with your Father - Adieu - God bless you - love to all inquiring Friends - run up to Pendleton with this when your Master gives you leave

J. S.

My Dearest Wife/
I have deferred writing unto you till his Day because it is our wedding Day, and this is the minute the rev'd James Archer joined our hands, and said among other Things "Those whom God hath joined together, let not man put asunder" My Heart thrills at the thought; look at the charming and healthy offspring we have raised; I cannot

look at them; I hope the Day is not distant when we shall meet to part no more; Pray God our Children may prove as virtuous Men and Women, as they are healthy and welformed - and my dear Hannah let you and I during the Remainder of our lives, endeavour to the utmost of our power to set them an example worthy of Imitation; if we do so endeavour I doubt not the almighty God will bless us; if not with wealth etc. in this World, he will Crown us with Peace, in "another and a better world than this."

I fervently hope and trust my Dear Wife and Children are in good Health; as for me I never enjoyed such health these thirty years during winter as I have done this; tho' winter is now set in, the natives say severely, to me it is nothing, we have a fire, a beautiful sky, and it is quite dry under foot. I have no wheezing in the Breast, not Cough at all, but quite as free, and clear as you used to be.

This morning I have been after a small Farm of 60 acres, which I mentioned in a former letter - there is a good House (a Tavern) and Summer Kitchen, water, etc. but the out Building is not good; the Rent is 100$ per year or (*unreadable word*). The distance from this city is 9 1/ 2 miles on a good Road - I shall enter upon it the 25th of next March conditionally - it is in the Jerseys, in a very pleasant neighborhood, where many English Families are located; I have been tempted to this proceeding by not receiving any encouragement to return to England. I should wish you & Family to come over with Mr. E. Grundy - I will write to him, and you again, by the first vessel which sails from N. York, - my bargain is not fairly concluded, but will be no doubt on Saturday next - I only rent it on this condition that I shall have the first privilege to purchase, when a good Title can be given and Terms agreed upon (abt. 2000$). Trade is going very well here at present as you will see by some of my late letters - when I think this is our wedding Day, my hand trembles worse than it did when I put the Ring upon your Finger.

Bowring, the Butcher, desires to be remembered to his Wife and Children, he frequently calls upon me, and often mentions them; he is now doing pretty well, and might do better; he has got about 60$. I think more; he can save 10$ per week very well when he pleases; My dearest Hannah I have scarcely room to give my Respects to Mr. Brettargh, Mr. Hamilton etc. and send my love, no I cannot send it. I cannot express it to you and my Dear Children, John, Hannah, Frances, Maria, Eliza, James & Joseph; God bless them, I often think of you and of them and count their names; You will see my letter to my Friends J. Brettargh and J. Bancroft which comes by the same Vessel - why do you not write to me - I have no letters, but those which Mr. F. Wrigley brought me - Adieu my dearest,
J. S. Jany. 9. 1821

P.S. give my love and respects to my old, my dear Mother, tell her not to grieve for me - I am well, very well - My Brothers and Sisters will gladly receive my Christmas Compliments I dare say - give them also to your Sister, Brother, Nephews etc. in Yorkshire - I wish your Sister and family were here - they would do well - I see amany people from Oldham, Royton, Middleton, Manchester etc. frequently.

Letter addressed to:
Mr. John Stott at Mr. Goadsby's, Chymist & Druggist, Chapel Street, Salford, Manchester
by the Packet Ship James Monroe from N. York to Liverpool

Chapter IV
Separation, Anxiety, and Decision

An Uneasy Heart

When, at the start of February, James still had received no further mail packets from England, the tone of his correspondence reflected his "uneasy heart" and inability to understand the lengthy silence from his family. His concern was tinged with self-righteous annoyance as he railed against the conditions in England, his feelings of isolation, and despair at having been "forsaken" by his loved ones.

It was in that state of mind that James made the fateful decision to rent (with an option to purchase) a farm and tavern and to send for Hannah and the children. With little preamble, he issued detailed instructions as to when his family should pack their belongings and set sail for America. James listed the supplies he expected them to transport and mentioned some of the conditions they might encounter during their ocean crossing. Leaving no question as to his expectation that his family would follow his directive, he told Hannah that he

would "have a man at the City waiting" for them to arrive.
Hannah's immediate reaction to that letter remains a mystery.

LETTER NINE

My dear Wife/
Time rolls on, another month is over since I last
addressed you, and our Son John, it was in the same letter;
I thought the same Postage would do; you know my dear
that money is not over-plentiful at present - I have not
ceased to write unto you since my arrival in this Country -
I have not ceased to think of you and our dear Children -
God bless them - since I left you. But pray wife, what am
I to think of you? Only one letter in so many months - one
solitary letter! This is not as it should be. I have fed upon
Hope until it is almost vanished - will Despair succeed? I
trust not - I feel my heart uneasy. When I ruminate - when
I reflect upon, and about my wife, my Children, my Relations
and my Friends, and though last mentioned, not least thought
of, my Country! I say I feel my heart uneasy. Ye whose
clay cold Hearts can forget all but their selfish selves, I
en(j)oy not your feelings! The Ship Amity is just arrived at
New York - what is the Ship Amity to me? not one line of
love from my Hannah, not one line from my Son - but why
have my Friends forsaken me? has the Frost bitten their
Fingers?
Are you so happy in the Land of your forefathers as to
imagine Happiness is chained to your Rock - chained did I
say - when I mentioned the word my Heart thrilled - Chains,
England - how do the names sound together? forbid it
Heaven that they should be long coupled - forbid it just
God! oh forbid it, that a Briton and a Slave should continue
to be used as synonimous Terms - Rather than bear the

worse than Egyptian Bondage in affluent Circumstances in Britain - in the land where a Hunt, a Knight, a Bamford etc. are incarcerated for defending the just Rights of the People, - I would live upon Sheeps Heads and Stale Bread[a] in a State of Freedom - my Heart grows warm - my feelings overpower me - I will lay down my Pen awhile. - Curse the Tyrants - nay not Curse them, I would not curse a Dog - but let me indignantly spurn them, before I drop the Pen. - what my Sons be slaves! and my Daughters be the Wives of Bondsmen. I hate the Thought.

Since writing the above (Feby. 2.) I have read some Extracts from the English Newspapers brought by the Amity - I see Sir Francis'[1] motion is overruled - but the Atty. General - kind Soul - does not wish him brought up for Judgment during the present Term - the sentence must hang in terrorism "to keep the Wretch in Awe." - the Parliament - pray what is that noise in St. Stephens? is it the roar of Party or is it the last Groan of Liberty? I see the Demons of Discord hovering around my native land - Envy and Calumny are sprouting Brimstone and Fire against the Radicals - Castlereagh and the Speaker shrouded in Conspiracy and attended by Corruption march from the "Den of Thieves" through the Lobby of Promotion to the House of "right Honourable Incurables." There they hear that (*unreadable word*) and Pensioners are ordered Home to read over Volumes of Sessions "on Conspiracy and Impurity," in order that their minds may be properly prepared for further Persecutions of - a Woman. Now they are met again - where does the Bill of Indemnity spring from? Will the pious Wilberforce[2] introduce it - hear how he laments the late exposure; how sorry he is that Royalty should have been laid so bare etc. etc. - wishes the whole could be buried in Oblivion - and the wounds and stabs of Virtue healed. Can the Friend of the Abolition of Black Slavery in a foreign land be sincere? Can you esteem his Philanthropy who can feel for Millions of Black Men whom he never saw, but who can chuckle and rejoice in the woes and wants of White Men who amid their privations and absolute wants, amid their vexatious persecutions, their illegal convictions, fines, and Imprisonment's, never opens his pious lips to vindicate them as men, nor his purse strings to relieve their wants and those of their suffering offspring! When Black men were driven to Crimes - even to murder; he said Cruel Taskmaster oppression, and want of Education, had driven them, goaded them on - to these cruel Deeds! but, the poor Soul can see no Cruel Taskmaster, no oppression in England, heigh-ho! away with politics for ever! I will think no more of the Tyrants. What can I forget my Country? nay - never - can I forget my poor old Mother, and Brothers and Sisters and Friends, and Relatives? no! - then I cannot forget their oppressors - I would I were something more than a railer against them. how the Nation rattled its Chains, when the Queen went to Saint Pauls! I am afraid the Vibrations would loosen the Stores of winter, and cause bad weather in the Land - Where is the Strong Ale and Spice Loaf and Cheese, Roast Beef and Christmas Pie, vanished to? Why, into the coffers of the Treasury.

Feby 3. We have delightful weather this week back - Well my dear Wife, not hearing anything from you, and seeing by the papers just arrived that another Game of Blood is going to be played in Europe, I have determined to have no Hand in it - I have taken the Farm about nine miles from this City in the State of New Jersey which I mentioned to you in my last letter; it contains from 60 to 70 Acres, with liberty to cut my own Fire wood, it is on a good Road in a pleasant neighborhood about 3 miles from Tide water amidst plenty of Fruit, Fish, Rabbits and other what is called Game in England - The Rent is 100$ per year - I think to purchase the Estate if I can get it for 1800$ and a suitable time allowed to pay for it.

I hope upon receipt of this you will immediately prepare to come over; and as I fully expect Mr. E. Grundy this Spring I trust he will have the kindness to protect you during the passage. You will see the impossibility of me fetching you as I intended, because I must enter upon my Farm the 25th of March next.

from one of my letters to Mr. Brettargh you will learn what Sea Stores to lay in - bring one Bushel of Peas with you - what are left we can sow - bring a Quart of Long pod Beans, and some flower Seeds - there are but few flowers raised in the Gardens in this Country - Bring all of my mathematical Books and Instruments as I intend keeping a School for 6 months each year to instruct our own Children and those of our English neighbors - what Books there are more than Forty Volumes, divide between my Son John and Daughters Hannah and Frances and put into their Boxes and call them theirs, else I shall have an import duty to pay - bring all your China, very carefully packed and knives, forks, and earthenware - bring all your bedding - bring the warming Pan - you can take the handle out and leave that - bring all my receipt Books including those I purchased from Mr. Foulkes - bring your best Fire Irons - and one set of common ones - bring Hammer and pincers - bring two or three Dozen of bottles Porter; You will find it best for you if Sea Sick upon your passage - bring one Cleaver and small Hatchet and Hand saw, chisels etc.

Bring bed curtains and those for the windows - bring flannel, it always sells very well here in Autumn - bring neither Silks nor Laces, they are very cheap here - purchase several old Boxes and get them numbered 1.2.3.4. etc. and keep an Inventory of what you have in each Box - Mr. Brettargh I dare say will draw it out for you - this will assist you in finding anything you want upon your passage - you must be sure to have one empty Box when you start to put your dirty linen in.

In respect to the Stores, its not be prevailed upon to bring much biscuit; 30 or 40 lb will be plenty for you all, bring a load of the best Potatoes you can purchase, what are left I shall plant in our Farm. Potatoes are not near so good here as they are with you - Farmers are not careful in setting good sorts. Bring the Frying pan from Home, you can get the Blacksmith to cut the handle so short as to go into a Box - bring some pretty strong nails to drive up on board to hang things on, and some length of line to stretch along side your birth to draw a curtain upon to skreen you when in bed - if Mr. Grundy be not coming this Spring, nor any other Friend that you can confide in; look around when you get on board for some civil, active, person, and agree to give him three or four Dollars to look after your Boxes etc. and to Cook and fetch and carry to the (*unreadable word*) or fire place for you, particularly in Stormy weather if you chance to have any, but perhaps you will not.

When Sea Sickness comes on, besure you dont give up to it too much, get up two or three times at least every Day, and walk about and sit upon Deck in the fresh air as long as you are able - then lie down and get upon Deck again etc. if you give up to lying in Bed, it is (*unreadable word*) you will be Sick during the whole passage, and that will be very bad for our Children.

The Children will feel little if any Sickness - let them run upon Deck and play whenever they think fit, be under no fear for them. be sure to lay in Sea Stores (have a Box for them etc. etc.) according to the instructions given in my letter alluded to above - look after your Boxes, your Provisions etc. etc. frequently during your passage - the Children's small Boxes may be stowed at their feet on the Bed, and perhaps one on your Bed, have the others nailed along side your Births which be sure to choose one over the other, and your largest Box along side you to use as a Table and a stepping Block to get into the higher birth - let the Girls sleep above you - bring Oatmeal and make porridge for the Children and let them have Molasses or Treacle[3] or Butter and Sugar to them - you can get Tea, Gruel etc. for yourself.

I expect you to Sail about the beginning of April and to arrive here in 30 to 40 Days after - besure you dont come in a vessel loaded with Salt if you can help it - such Ships sail very heavy and make long passages - come in a regular Trader to Philadelphia, for if you land at New York, is will cost us as much to get you home as it will to bring you there - write me letter by the Packet which leaves Liverpool the first of April and tell me the Ship's name you intend to come in and the Day you purpose sailing, I will have a man at the City waiting for you when your arrive - then I will fly to meet you and our Dear Children - happy moment, how I anticipate it - to meet my Dearest in a Land of Liberty. Perhaps my dear friends J.B. & J. B. are coming this Spring as they do not write to me - I wish they were I could find good Farms and cheap in the neighbourhood of mine - which is amongst Friends or Quakers; at Haddonfield (abt. 3 m. off) is a very very large meeting, and sheds for a hundred Horses at least.

English Farmers when they arrive here generally find themselves disappointed - They expect to find fine green rich pasture fields - here are very few green fields indeed - the Cows etc. run in the woods during Summer, and are fed, milked etc. as I have mentioned in my former letters - a great many Farmer are arrived from the West and South of England in this Country this Autumn and winter. They appear dissatisfied, so many of them will go into the backwoods - alas they will be unhappy there - the Truth is Things are here at present as they used to be in England abt 60 to 70 years back - here is ease and plenty - not plenty of money - women spin upon one spindle - they knit - they sew- the men plow - reap - go to market etc. and in winter in the Country - they spend their evenings in cracking Nuts, eating apples, drinking Cider, and talking of bad Times - in the Cities there is more wickedness - a poor man who has not a yard of land may keep a Cow or two if he lives a few miles from the City - he buys Hay & Corn for them in the winter and in summer turns them out, and they fend for themselves.

I mentioned in my last letter that the place I had in view was a Farm and Tavern - but my dear do not understand that a Country Tavern here is similar to the Country Tavern with you - there is not sitting down to drink in the country here - the people just call for a glass - stand at the Bar to drink it - and away they go - they are afraid of being called sots if they sit down to drink.

I am writing to my Friends J. B. and J. B. and expect they will read you the letter which may perhaps give some particulars not mentioned here - I shall direct this to Son John as usual and hope he will have the goodness to deliver it the first opportunity - you will hear from my letter to Mr. E. Grundy what severe weather the Americans say we have had here but it has been very fine these last 12 Days - in fact we have only had two cold Days it is almost always dry both overhead and under foot - the river is frozen up at present which makes things rather dull in the city tho' both Cotton ad Woollen trade goes well - yea very well at present - Love to Friends and all my Relations - I send a Kiss to each of our Children- God bless them - little Joseph can call dad dad etc. by this time I suppose and James you will have in boys Dress - I shall hardly know him - accept of my true love - your faithfully
J.S. Feby. 6. 1821.

Note written along the left hand margin of the third page:

In respect to money matters, I wrote to Brother William at Xmas
- and I shall say more upon the Subject in my letter to Friends J. B.
and J. B. Tis passing strange that not one friend will write to me! -
surely my letters are suffered to pass - we shall soon meet I hope
and then you can explain all these mysteries to me - I never enjoyed
better Health than at present - M. Walker's family are all well

Note written along the left hand margin of the last page:
Bowring the Butcher has spent all his money - he has been having
a fuddle and nearly just taken up and bought 9 sheep. I am afraid he
is in a bad way again - dont mention this to his wife

[a]what we here call Boston Crackers, or buttered Crackers are a
good thing to take on Ship board

Letter addressed to:
Mr. John Stott at Mr. Goadsby's, Chymist Druggist, Chapel Street
Salford, Manchester

[1]*Sir Francis probably referred to Sir Francis Burdett, a member
of the Oppostion in the House of Commons who was active in
promoting Parliamentary reform (Halevy 150). Following the
Manchester Meeting, Sir Francis wrote a strong letter denouncing
the use of the yeomanry and threatened the King with the fate of
James II (Halevy 65) who was exiled by his unhappy subjects.*

[2]*The evangelical British abolitionist, William Wilberforce, was
active in the Anti-Slave Trade Committees that led to the end of
slave trade in England in 1807 and finally to slavery itself in
1833. Motivated by his belief that policitics must adhere to the
tenets of Christianity (Trevelyan 51-53), in 1812, Wilberforce
and other philanthropists founded the Association for Relief of
the Manufacturing & Labouring Poor in reaction the economic
problems in the country (Halevy 12).*

[3]"Treacle" originally was used as a term designating a remedy for poison, but in England was used to refer to molasses.

Following that last communication to Hannah, James had little choice but to wait and trust that she and the children would receive his letter, accede to his wishes, and set sail for America. During that period, he was kept busy settling the farm and managing the tavern.

LETTER TEN

White Horse Tavern[a] Apl 6. 1821

Dear Son/
I began a letter to you about a month back, which owing to Disappointments in relation to disposing of my Stock etc. in South Street I had not time to compleat - I hope and trust you received my letter of Jany. and Feby. safe - two directed for you, dated Feby. 8 or 9 and one to Mr. E. Grundy at the same Time. I think, John, that you and Friends have not received half the letters I have written; and perhaps I have not received all you answers. My Troubles will be great indeed if the letters of Feby. have not been delivered - I expect your Dear Mother and Sisters etc. are coming to me - I will know you have too much good Sense to grieve at the loss of them - remember it is only temporary (I mean your separation)
The Sun, I beguile the tedious hours with thinking, has risen in England, when it is on the Meridian I will return if living - if dead, my Children will - I trust in God they will - but Son, if I die here you will have the Consolation of knowing that the Bones of your Father rest in the Earth of

Liberty and that I trust will be no small gratification to your mind - If God would grant my Choice, I would rather that my Tomb should be in the Rattle Snakes Den, then that my Dust should be mingled with that of the Boroughmonger's. - The rattle snake only bites when necessity compels him to the Act - The Boroughmongers prey upon the Vitals of the Poor; Are the poor devoured? Then you rusty headed sons of Curly headed Sires, ye clodhoppers, beware! or the Vultures will prey upon your Livers!

I removed to this place on the 26th (*unreadable word*) and am now busy in my Farm - I have got Hens and Turkeys etc. Mr. Kinsey,[b] whose Son is well known to Mr. Bancroft, is a very near neighbour of mine - I have only about 6 or 8 Acres to cultivate this Summer, the remaining part is sown with Rye (in Autumn) and is meadows & wood land - I intend to plant Indian Corn and potatoes and Turnips in the land I have at liberty. I have a man Servant and woman Servant, or they are here called Helps, but my female Help is no Assistance. I am going to part with her, because she Helps herself too much in the Gin Keg!

Oh! how I long for your Dear Mother and Sisters and Brothers! - every week now feels a month and every month a couple of years and more - your letter on Jany. 30 is just come to hand, and so is that of our good Friend J. Brettargh - I kindly thank you both; your Mother advises me not to lay in too great a Stock of Spirits, but upon my word I never had more occasion for them than at present - you will see by my last letter how cheap I sell them but I cannot purchase any of the kind I want - perhaps I want not Spirits - no tis only the Balsam of Domestic Comfort that can soothe the perturbed Bosom of your affectionate Father - Son, do not mourn - do not grieve - mind the Counsel which I gave you in my letter of Xmas last - I received the packet of letters and Newspapers which you mention on or about the 16th of Feby - tell the doctor, whom you allude to that he may safely place his money out at 6 per Cent Int. or he may place it in the Funds, and in respect to a Situation of few miles from the City he may get one both elegant and Convenient at a very low rent.

Provisions are now very low - I purchased at the City when I came over here, a Barrel of excellent wheat Flour and another of Rye, each weighing 196 lbs. The wheat flour cost me 3.50 Dollars and the rye 1.75 Dollars, both together 5.25$! I purchased corned Beef at 5 Cents per lb. and fresh Pork at the same price - Sugar is from 8 to 12 1/2 Cents per lb. butter according to Quality from 12 1/2 to 25 Cents, but not much so high - Coffee 25 to 28 Cents - Lump Sugars 15 to 18 Cents per lb. good Tea .85 to 1.00$ per lb. - but now John calculate that I shall have to sell in the same proportion that I buy - I intend to keep a School for 6 months at least out of the 12 and as there is no School near I think I can make it answer pretty well - at least it will have the advantage I can instruct you Sisters and Brothers

I intend to write to our respected friends J.B. & J.B. by this packet if possible, but on account of Time being short and Distance from the post something; and being engaged in looking after a Home - plough - waggon - business etc. I do not know that I shall have Time - but I will steal so much if possible - I hope our good friend Mr. E. Grundy is coming along in the same Ship with your Dear Mother etc. as I mentioned, and will strive to make her comfortable - if not I dare say you will remember the advice which I gave in one of my letters for Persons to engage a likely man to cook etc. for them during the whole voyage for a certain Sum of money - say five Dollars for your Family - but this of course is over and they are at this Date buffeting the waves of the Atlantic, which are not half so terrible in proof as they are in Tales told to the timid in England

I have written a very particular letter to Mr. Brettargh

on the subject of Mr. Howarth's Coal Plan (the Date was Feby. 27th- I think) I could set them at right in 2 Days, but I left everything with Brother Wm and full Information upon the Subject - if they send them over they had better keep duplicates - but I must have both the Plans and Dimension Books - and the Duplicates or else I can do nothing with them - enough; I told Mr. B. the whole before - In respect to Brother Thomas I have written two letters to him and have not received any answer - in them I gave him every explanatory Satisfaction - I am truly sorry that Mr. A. Knowles has not gotten the letter which I sent him - they are filled with Sketches of the Different strata in several States; together with various Geological observations - I think none of those letters (*unreadable word*) of all which I have written to all my Friends from America - I would not take 100$ for their contents.

I hope your Dear Mother would take care and lay in sufficient Sea Stores according to Directions given - and as this is a very pleasant Season of the year I expect they will have a comfortable passage - in my last letter I gave you the Particulars of my Situation in some Respects, but intend to give you as small Sketch of it in my next - there is a beautiful mill seat near to my Farm which Mr. & Mrs. F. Wrigley have been to view - it was sold (*unreadable word*) on Saturday last for 7050$. There are 260 Acres of land belonging to it - besides considerable Buildings and a very powerful stream of water 14 feet fall - land is certainly very low and much is upon Sale - when the war with England made money plentiful, Farmers mortgaged their lands - spent the money, and have never since been able to pay it back owing to Peace and low prices - generally speaking the Americans are anxious for a European War - or rather for a War in Europe - Trade goes well and working men's wages are high.

(In the original letter, the remaining text was

superimposed on the lines comprising the previous two pages, but written across at an angle of ninety degrees. While this made reading slightly more difficult, most words were still clearly legible.)

Manufactures - English woollen goods and hardware sell very low at auction - Domestic goods are very much encouraged - even Domestic coffee is commonly used in the best Taverns - there is much rivalry and jealousy between the different States - in Time there will be a division of them - called Eastern and Western Unions of Columbia or some other which the sons of Liberty may like better.

I was at (*unreadable word*) yesterday and Judge Firth who was holding a Court there hearing I was in the House left his Bench, came and shook Hands with me, and gave me a very cordial Invitation to his House etc. It would not be so in England - Squires and Judges frequently call upon one here - they are more familiar then usually Attorney's are in England- one of them told me last Evening that he would make up a Small party and come and take a Beef Steak with me in the course of a few Weeks - They are chiefly wealthy Farmers -   The land in the Jerseys is much run down in Philadelphia etc. but our Farmers generally reply by showing them our produce - no Country in the World produces finer Corn, Pork, or Beef and in respect to Poultry we are compleatly without a rival - Pompions, Cucumbers, Melons, water Melons, Gourds etc. grow almost without Invitation; upon which Cows are principally fed during the hot months. In this Country the Cows have Salt twice each day in the Summer and frequently during the Winter- generally speaking the Farmers here are either ignorant or negligent of their Business - we have too much land under the Plough.

I will send Brother William a Design or the Pretty writing piece in my next letter to him. The original is hanging up in the Merchants Coffee House in the City where I have got liberty to take a copy

Apl.7. at noon - since writing the above I have purchased 2 Horses and Saddle and Bridle for 10 dollars. In England they would have fetched at least 70 Pounds Sterling since I left - one of them is to plow and draw a light waggon - the other is a (*unreadable word*) beautiful brown pony abt 13 1/2 Hands high - playful and full of action as a young Lamb - gently to ride and well conditioned he will just suit your sister Frances - Hannah will be afraid to mount I dare say - you must suppose I am in a very handsome neighborhood - among amine English people.

give my Kind love to your Master - be sure to be obedient and industrious - I would not hurt your feelings by mentioning Honesty - Direct in future for me to be left at the post office Philadelphia till called for - and do my Dear Son write by every Packet which Sails from Liverpool - I cannot write this post to my Esteemed friends B. and J. B. do give my warmest Love and thanks to them - Farms, say to J. Bancroft are going low - he might suit himself I am certain - give my Love to my Dear old Mother and Brothers and Sisters and to all inquiring friends - do not encourage your Aunt to call upon you - adieu dear Son- God bless you - pray for him who always prays for you - dont forget your Brothers and Sisters etc. - The man who takes this ltr is waiting - more in my next.

J. Stott

Notes written along the left margin of the first page referring to James' flagged sentences

[a]White Horse Tavern is in the county and township of Gloucester abt. 9 miles from the Ferry at Camden opposite Philadelphia-

[b]he is anxiously expecting a letter and 400$ from his Son - mention this to Mr. Bancroft

Note written on the address page
excuse all inaccuracies you will - the haste it has been written in
- I have not had Time to read it over

Letter addressed to:
Mr. John Stott at Mr. Goadsby's, Chymist & Druggist
Chapel Street, Salford, Manchester
to go by the regular Packet from N. York to Liverpool which sails
the 10th April 1821.

The next piece of sequential correspondence is a letter from James'
son John to his Uncle William (James' brother), both of whom were
residing in England. James had no knowledge of this communication
in which there is confirmation that Hannah, heeding James'
instructions, had indeed set sail for America.

LETTER ELEVEN

begun Sunday, 15 Apl. 1821.

Dear Uncle/
I recd. my clothes safe together with your Most tender
and Affectionate of ltrs; what words must I use to express
the Grateful feelings of my Heart, Words are too weak to
express the gratitude I feel for you and my dear Aunt, were
I with you I could kiss you both a Bath your thanks with the
tears of thankfulness as I can make another return at
present. I am obliged to you for the arrangement you have
made respecting my Clothes.
My feelings dear Uncle have been tortured this last

week & my Anxiety is not yet (*unreadable word*) for the Safe arrival of my dear Mother, Brothers, Sisters in America & their happy meeting with my Father. Then "what Tongue can tell how great their Joy shall be."

(Wednesday Night). To give you now what information I have had. Mr. Brettargh returned from Lpool on Saturday the 7th. (*unreadable word*) he called at our shop on Monday the 9th & told me when My Mother, Brothers, Sister arrived at Lpool on Tuesday the captain had postponed sailing until the 7th or 8th. on account of the Rough Weather. He left Lpool at 2 o'clock on Saturday afternoon & they expected to weigh anchor at 5. Mr. Bancroft did not go to Lpool until Friday the 6th having read a ltr stating the postponement. he returned on Wednesday the 11th called at our Shop on Thursday told me they got no farther than the Rock on Saturday. on Sunday the 8th no Breeze. on Monday owing to the negligence of the Pilot they could not get out. upward of 50 vessels sailed this morning.

on Tuesday the 10th very Stormy dared not attempt. on Wednesday the 11th the Pilot weighed anchor too late & after a fruitless effort they were forced to cast anchor again. left Lpool at 10 o'clock today as he could stop no longer. having Slept two nights on board purposely to see them sail. on Saturday recd. a ltr from his Son dated Thursday the 12th. he Says the Captain was very much dissatisfied with the Pilot on Wednesday & sent him on Shore & procured another who took advantage of the fair Wind on Thursday Morn at 5 o'clock, weighed Anchor & set sail at 7 o'clock the Hour this letter is dated they were in sight of the Welsh Mountains & the Pilot just leaving them.

They were all in excellent Health & Spirits although Joseph had been ill whilst at Lpool/except Mr. Corbett's youngest daughter who was sea sick all ready. There was only 2 Cabin passengers one a young Physician whom a friend of Mr. Bancroft knew & introduced him to Mr. Corbett & Daughter & my Dear Mother & who promis'd to render them any Medical assistance in his power they might require.

My first employment in a Morning is to look which way the Wind blows & to think how far each succeeding Day bears. I cannot say all my hopes of happiness away though my dearest and nearest relations.

To my dear Uncle & Aunt whilst I have you left I cannot say so Robt. Knowles has called & says his Father & Mother desire that I would make it convenient to go there as often as possible, Mr. & Mrs. Brettargh the same Mr. Williamson of Fathers (*unreadable*) the same. if a fine Sunday I hope to get leave on the 29th to come a seeing you

let me ask you dear Uncle what I can fill a ltr with each month my wants are not so many yet let me ask myself am I perfect in every thing. My Answer is no though my Worldly wants are few. wants of more importance I have amany.

I am very much obliged to my dear Aunt for the arrangement of my Clothes & for the hours She has taken to plate the Ruffle of my fine shirt but as they are at this time more plain by most respectable Persons I should be very sorry to give her so much unnecessary trouble. I wear Night Shirts which I suppose you did not know of & Dirty one for fortnight. This week I shall be employed in writing to my dear Father as I intend to say the favor of Mr. E. Grundy taking it. He sails on the 7th of May. I complete this ltr with my most grateful thanks to you & my dear Aunt & hoping to have the pleasure of seeing you on Sunday next I remain your very lov'g & affectionate Nephew

J. Stott

Letter addressed (for hand delivery) to:
Uncle Wm. Stott
Apl. 1821

Hannah and the Children

As James began the process of establishing his farm in New Jersey, the whereabouts of his family was completely unknown to him. It seems safe to assume from his past expressions of apprehension concerning their well-being, he must have been extremely worried about them. However, rather than filling his monthly letter to his son with questions and speculations about the family, James was uncharacteristically silent on the subject. One can reasonably theorize that he was not allowing himself to focus on the enormity of his decision to send for Hannah and the children.

In this next correspondence to John dated May 6, 1821, the texture of James' writing can best be portrayed as "nervous chatter." The introduction, unlike any of his previous thoughtful communications, was decidedly prosaic. He followed that first portion with an extremely detailed recitation of his methods of planting. Then, for little apparent reason, James inserted a copied paragraph concerning the counterfeiting of money along the Canadian border.

Finally, on May 14, before completing the letter, James received word about Hannah and his sons and daughters. From that point on the tone of his discourse changed. Phrases were written hurriedly with thoughts tripping over one another in his excitement and eagerness to tell John about the docking of the ship *Warren*.

LETTER TWELVE

Gloucester Township, & County N.J.
May 6, 1821

My dear Son/
Another month has rolled over since I last wrote to you
and little or nothing new has occurred to me, worthy of
transplanting to Europe - I remember my promise of writing
regularly each month, to you or to some of my Friends and
therefore I will fulfill it. I have just sent off two letters, one
to Mr. Brettargh and the other to Mr. Bancroft, which letters
I hope you will have the pleasure of perusing, they contain
several particulars which I have mentioned in some of my
former letters, or at least I have mentioned the same Subjects
before, but not perhaps the same particulars. If any of them
appear to clash with what I have before written, it is thus
accounted for "I always describe Things as they appear to
me at some particular place and Time, or as they are
represented generally to me by oral Information which I
can rely upon or by the News."
    In my last letter to Friend Brettargh I mentioned the
planting etc. of Indian Corn, in which I described the rows
to be five foot by four foot apart, this was a trifling Error,
as I find by experience the rows are five foot apart - a
small spade full of manure is put into each Hill, on which
are carefully thrown three, four, or five grains of Corn,
after a little steeping in clear water and being rolled in plaster
of paris ground fine - which (plaster) is thought to invigorate
the Plants much, when they grow up -- it does most certainly
contain a considerable portion of the Sulphate of Lime which
attracts the moisture of the atmosphere and by that means
keeps the land moist, which will certainly, in this dry climate
assist the growth of vegetables, particularly during the dry

nights. A good, full grown Ear of Corn contains from 4 to 700 grains - about 750 or 800 grains of good corn will be a pint - and you will, by Calculation, find that if a pint only grows upon one Hill, there will be about 27 Bushels upon a Statute Acre. Of course a Quart upon a Hill will be upwards of 50 Bushels to the Acre which is here called a good Crop.

Among the Corn are Sewn Pomkins, Melons, Cucumbers, etc. The Pomkins weigh from 10 to 60 or 70 lbs each. The water melons grow to a larger size, I have seen amany larger than two Gallon Bottle - the Cucumbers are of various sizes, but upon an average they are larger and more numerous by far than they are in England.

Besides the Corn, a Farmer will raise here, off good land, from 1 1/2 to 3 Tons weight of the above described Truck (as such things are here called)) with which they feed Hogs, Cows, and Horses. All animals are particularly partial to Salt, in this Country, and it is said they could not live long without it - even the wild Cattle find, what are called Salt Licks, and it is proved that Deer will go 10 or 15 miles to drink at one of them - near to such Places the Hunter be in ambuscade to shoot them.

I am now sowing Cucumbers, water melon, Pomkins, etc. We sow them in Hills after the same plan nearly that we sow Corn - among the different Seeds we plant Potatoes. Thus, the rows are laid out as under, four feet asunder and the Hills are four feet apart, so that the Cucumbers Hills, Pomkins etc. are just eight feet distant, and so are the Potatoes.

We put a small portion of good Dung in each Hill or point as represented above (*sketch not reproducible*), but none between them - and act just in a similar manner when we plant among the Corn as aforementioned. I do not intend to plant amongst my Corn this Season, because I have not manure enough - I do think to sow Turnip Seed in a part of it, if I can get the ground into proper condition.

When your Ground is run out with continual working, we then plough and sow it with what we call Indian Peas, which pea is a native of this Country, having been found in it when Columbus first discover the land. This Pea is of a yellow grey colour and something resembling the English Vetch in shape, but considerably larger - I like these peas very well, when boiled in Soup - they sell from a Dollar to $1.30 per Bushel.

I have but a small Orchard upon my Plantation; the Trees are growing rather old; I can make the apples if the Season is favourable about 20 Barrels of Cider; I have only two Pear Trees; there is a considerable number of Cherry Trees, some of the Fruit of which will be ripe about the beginning of June - the Cherries are now as large as a small Pea.

We have great variety of curious and beautiful Flowers growing wild in our Wood besides the Flowering Shrubs, but we have no Primroses - we have what the Natives call the Honeysuckle, it is as handsome as yours in England but far from being as Fragrant

We have a great variety of Turtles. One is called the Snapping Turtle, some of them are named Terrapins, some Land Turtles, others they call Mud Turtles and soforth.

That you may have an Idea of the Quantity of bad money passing in some of the northern States of the Union, I give you the following extract of a Letter I was permitted to copy,

"The land which composed Grand Isle county is of the first Quality in the State of Vermont, - at the Tavern on this Island the Landlord would only take three kinds of money; Burlington, the Bank of Canada, and Bank of Montreal, which he said were the only notes that would pass. This is a striking Instance of the bad affect of counterfeit money, which will, if not stopped, finally stop all Trade in this part of the country. There is a large manufactory of this deceptive Paper in the edge of Canada, just over our Lines in which five or six Persons are employed constantly; People come from the States and purchase any amount they please at so much per cent. The Sellers of this Ruination call it Pictures. The Question is what will you take per hundred for your first, second or third rate Picture? One kind they sell at ten another at 15 Dollars per hundred; The above mentioned, or rather alluded to, Gentlemen counterfeited some notes on the Montreal Bank so perfectly that the Clerks took in 500$ before they discovered it to be counterfeit. There are but few of the Canadians that can read or write in these parts, and they are so affraid of being cheated again that they will receive nothing but hard money for their produce when they take it to market. As the above manufactory is in Canada the States people have no right to break it up; and as the Gentlemen sell the Pictures at so much per hundred, as Pictures and not as money, the English Governor has no Law to put them down - he has not power over them."

Query, do not these same Gentlemen manufacture Bank of England Notes? for they are much easier to be copied than any which I have seen in this Country; it would be easy to convey them to England by the idle and dissolute emigrants who return to that ill-fated Island.

May 14. I have just received a letter by the Amity that your dear Mother and brothers and sisters are coming by the Warren. Capt. Webb, the Amity, it appears left the Warren ready to sail, so that I expect my Comforts in, every Day? Thank God for all his Goodness. I will reserve the remainder of this sheet till they arrive

Monday 21st. 2 P.M. a messenger arrived to let me know that the Ship Warren is in the River - my Horses from Home could not start off immediately - at 8 P.M. met Daughter Frances in the Market Street, Philadelphia - She told me they came ashore at 5 o'clock all well; was very glad to hear it - her Mother and Sisters etc. at a Friends House more than a mile off - I soon found them.

Tuesday 22nd. after Breakfast we went aboard to look after luggage[1] - saw John Bankcroft Jr. & Mr. Corbett, both very well - had not time nor opportunity to have discourse with them - very busy till near Six getting luggage out of the Hold - examing by custom House officer etc. - had nothing to pay Duty for - officers civil - and so was I to them - sent luggage across the River - went and saw my wife - I forget to observe that Joseph is surely the prettiest Boy I very saw, there is something so charming, delightful, and pleasant in his Countenance; James is much improved - he did not know me at first - my Daughters all look well - Hannah is much improved in her Health - she is very tall - Frances stood Voyage best of any Passengers aboard - was not sick half an Hour - my dear Wife was much more comfortable and healthy than she expected - Joe was not sick at all - they tell me that a Welsh woman was delivered of a Son on the Banks of Newfoundland -She is for calling it Warren after the Ship it was born in. She is doing very well.

At evening left my Family in Town and went Home to fetch a waggon for luggage - a Dearborn for my Family - wet night - Wed. morning very wet - but shall go and bring all Home toDay - the Ship Lancaster is sailing this morning and I intend to send this letter by her to Liverpool. A many English People are coming with her upon Business, but none from Manchester - Mrs. Whittaker of Royton is one Passenger and Mr. Butterworth a Tin plate worker, who has a Store in Market between 3rd and 6th is another, he is coming to Oldham upon Business and will soon return. I haven't time for many words more. I must be going.

I have lately sent two letters to Mr. Brettargh and one to Mr. Bancroft - Mr. Grundy's last letter has never (*unreadable word*) to hand - I have one part written to my dear Brother William but not finish is at present - I know your good sense will teach you to be easy and trust that your virtuous Principles will teach you prudence - I should much like you to be mindful and attentive to your Business; strive by every just means to improve yourself in Knowledge of all Kinds; be a little, not over, inquisitive in learning the Secrets of your own Profession - treat your Master with marked civility and Respect - be civil and kind to his son - give my Respects to them both with best Respects to your dear Grandmother, Uncles, Aunts etc. and to (*unreadable word*) each friend (*unreadable words*). I am my dear Son your most loving and Affectionate father.

James Stott.

You may be sure that your Dear Mother and Sisters send their Love to you - and likewise to all friends particularly Mr. and Mrs. Brettargh and Family - your Sisters will write to you and other friends shortly after they are Settled and give you an account of their Voyage etc. - they are all much the same as when I left them, only improved - Adieu - I could write all Day to you, but I must be going for your Dear Mother etc. etc. - it still rains - but I will start off - my Indian Corn etc. is coming up well - oh! what a number of things I have forgot to tell you. They had a voyage of 37 Days Pilot to Pilot

Letter addressed to:
Mr. John Stott, at Mr. Goadsby's
Chymist & Druggist, Chapel St.
Salford, Manchester

Single sheet.
to be delivered

[1]*According to the Passenger List of the Ship Warren, Hannah and the children's baggage consisted of 9 trunks, 1 package, goods, 2 beds, and bedding (National Archives, M-425, Roll 31).*

Chapter V
In Transition

At Home in New Jersey

The sixty acre farm and tavern to which James brought Hannah and the children was located in Gloucester Township, an area of about 60,000 acres across the Delaware River from Philadelphia. Its population in 1820 was listed as 2029. The northern area was cultivated, for the most part, in vegetables and fruit while the southern section of the township consisted of mainly pine woods, providing a valuable resource for timber and fuel (Gordon [b] p. 149).

When daughter Hannah stated "it is country indeed," she was entirely accurate. According to James, the closest towns were Clementon and Haddonfield. Clementon, about two miles distant, was a small village with some twelve to fifteen dwellings (Gordon [b] 121), and Haddonfield, five miles from the Stott farm, was only somewhat larger. Its rich soil and proximity to the Philadelphia market made it a prime farming community (Gordon [b] 154).

Living in what was essentially a rural area must have felt very much like a pioneer existence to Hannah. Although nearby

Philadelphia was an established, cultured city, the Stott farm and its surroundings were comparatively primitive. Hannah, used to the more gentile life as the spouse of a mining engineer, suddenly found herself hauling water, tending livestock, and traveling the nine miles to Philadelphia at regular intervals to sell the Stott produce. In Philadelphia, the primary market was located on High Street and extended almost 4000 feet from the Delaware River to Eighth Street. The arriving farmers turned their wagons into temporary stalls, often spreading another 4000 feet on either side of the road. Second Street was the sight of another major market, stretching almost a mile in length, and additional smaller markets dotted the city (Gordon [a] pp. 365-366). Along with providing an outlet for selling their harvests, the markets afforded farmers the opportunity of meeting with one another and sharing experiences. Those journeys to Philadelphia proved to be an agreeable diversion for Hannah, as she was able to spend time with fellow British expatriates in their urban homes.

This next communication from the Stott's was written by James and Hannah's eldest daughter, Hannah. Just one month shy of her thirteenth birthday, Hannah penned a letter to her brother John relating some of the family's experiences during their ocean voyage and providing insights into her first impressions of life in America.

LETTER THIRTEEN

Dear Brother John/

I dare say will be anxious to hear from us, and as the Ship we sailed in is reported to return on the 10th Inst. to Liverpool, I should like this to go by her; we had a very comfortable Captain the sailors too were a set of kind steady men. Little Joseph was admired and beloved by all on board, he was in good health all the way, and improved very much, the Chief Mate loved him so well that he nursed him all he could, and Joseph loved him, and would leave his Mother to go to him, he used to come below in rough weather on purpose to nurse him. I was very sick three or four days and always sick when the weather was rough, John Bancroft fretted a few days. Mr. Corbett told him he was mammy Sick, he promised to come over to see us but has not been yet, we believe he is in the City, and have heard that he is for working. Sister Francis would have kept a Journal but she had not time, she was always upon deck, in another voyage or two she would be almost able to command a ship.

We were running up the river Delaware before a fine breeze on Sunday afternoon at the rate of ten miles an hour, and thought to be in port at eight o'clock but behold when we were within two miles of the City we were struck on a bank of mud and stuck fast till Monday noon, this was one of our greatest disappointments we could see the City but could not approach. For about a Hundred miles up the Delaware the scene was beautiful. New Jersey on one side, and pennsilvania on the other it appeared enchanting to us after our voyage. The woods and orchards looked delightful the farm houses are chiefly built of wood some of them were painted red and others white.

We got into the city about 5 o'clock in the afternoon. A person came on board and inquired for us we took a little boat and went on shore she took us to Mr. Hill's House who is a Yorkshire Man he lives in Market Street, we there met with Mr. F. Rigby and several other Gentlemen from England who knew my Father. They were glad to see us, we admired the City much, there are fine stately poplars growing on each side the streets we went by the Hospital which is a beautiful building there are lemon and orange trees with fruit upon them growing round the grass plat in front of the hall and a Statue of William Penn stands in middle of it.

One Mr. Wilson let my Father know that we was come

the same day we arrived we had not been long at Mr. Hill's before a Mr. Megran who had been to see my Father called and took as many of us as he could in a gig to his house where we stopped all night my Father got to the City about 8 o'clock the same evening we were all very glad to see him. James did not know him at first but soon got friends with him he was very glad to see us and very well pleased with little Joseph next morning we had for breakfast a variety of dishes on the table there was tea, coffee, ham, and eggs, cold fowl, dryed beef, cheese & butter and bread. We stopt there till wednesday, then my Father fetched us home.

As we went through the woods we admired the vines running up the trees as high as Mr. Goadsby's house, there are amany shrubs here which do not grow in England, there are ten sorts of Oak. My Father finds an increase in his family in many a respect we have a Cow and calf, two good horses, two young pigs, a dog, and I think about 60 fowls altogether, there is ducks, hens, rooster, chickins, and amany young turkeys, with turkey hen and Gobler, it is not much trouble to rear fowls or anything here.

We have not yet been to any school but my Father intends opening one on munday next he has taken a room about half a mile from our house we shall go as amany of us as can be spared.

You will expect to know how we like the country; it is country indeed we are 9 miles from the City there is plenty of wood and amany sassafras trees growing in our land, we have amany Cherry trees and Apple, and pear, and Walnut trees in abundance. I think we shall have many a Waggon load of Apples. There is a great deal of Cedar about here, our Churn, milk pails, washing tubs, etc. are all made of Cedar wood. As to liking the country we like it very well but my Mother would have liked it better if we had been nearer the City.

There are strawberries here which grow in the Woods and fields, nearly as large a Garden Strawberries in England. My Father took the dimension of an oak leaf it was 12 6/10 Inches long and 10 7/10 Inches broad this sort is called black Oak. We have no cuckoos here, but we have a bird it seems to be about the size of a lark, which cries wip-pur-will, or wip-poor-will. there is the Tree frog here which will climb a very high tree, and there it sings or make its noise when it is going to rain.

My Mother send her respects to Mr. and Mrs. Baker and is much obliged to him for packing as we had nothing broke but one tumbler glass and that was done by putting too many one in another My Father and Mother sends their respects to Mr. and Mrs. Livingston and tell them we like the country pretty well we have seen Mr. and Mrs. Walker they send their respects to Mr. Lee, Mr. Hamilton, yourself and all other friends Mrs. Sidebotham is not very well she is uneasy about her Husband as they have not heard from him this long while they are affraid something is happened to him she was well pleased with the small present Mrs. Lee sent her she also joins her respects with Mr. and Mrs. Walker.

My Father and Mother sent their respect to Mr. and Mrs. Bancroft and family also to Mr. and Mrs. Brettargh and their family and tell them we are all very well in health, little Joseph is improved a great deal since he came here he can nearly walk he would have done before now but his was kept back on shipboard, they call him the ornament of the neighbourhood here. We have hear John Bancroft is got into work and can get 10 dollars a week (*Unreadable word*) berries are now beginning to be ripe, they are like wimberries in England. We shall have many a thousand of them. We did not use half the medicine we took with us we all join in best respects to Mr. and Mrs. Goadsby, and family.

We are grateful to him for all favours. I conclude Dear Brother with kind love to you and all friends. I remain
my Dear Brother John
your very affectionate sister
Hannah Stott
White Horse Gloucester Township
June 23rd. 1821
PS Please to look after your skates my Mother left them in the house she left on the shelf under the stairs she mentioned them to Uncle William to look after them.
Sister Frances is writing to Miss Ashworth you will get to see her letter.

Note written by Hannah along the left hand margin of the first page:
You will please to mention us to all friends at Middleton, particulary your old Dear Grandmother & Family

Note written by Hannah along the left hand margin of the third page:
You will please to give my Mothers kind love to James Diggles family and to Mrs. Hamilton and Emily

Note written by James along the left hand margin of the third page:
Dear Son please to excuse the many mistakes and so on, which your Sister has made, and correct them; I have been busy planting Potatoes and have not had Time to attend to her as I otherwise should have done. We are all well - Direct to the post office Philadelphia - Mr. E. Grundy and family are not yet arrived.

Note written by James along the top margin of the last page:
Your Sisters and Mother desire their Respects to Mrs. & Miss Alice Williamson of Foster's Wood.

Letter addressed to:
Mr. John Stott
at Mr. Goadsby's
Chymist & Druggist, Salford, Manchester.

Ramifications

For the Stotts, establishing a home in an unfamiliar environment presented numerous challenges. The problems they encountered were unique and very different from those with which they had dealt in England. With his family now in residence, affairs in James' native land must have begun to seem increasingly distant. The emigration of Hannah and the children abruptly altered James' status from that of "temporary absentee" to one of "settler."

The permanency of the Stott situation suddenly took on a new reality for family members remaining in England. Some of the consequences of that reality were vividly revealed when James' brother William corresponded with him in June. William was the person left to deal with issues involving James' financial matters, family obligations, and professional duties. His resentment was palpable. That William felt obligated to pay for the "arrears" owed by James to his various clubs and answer for his neglected mining plans was extremely upsetting to him. Although many of the references to the various responsibilities are difficult to understand, William left no doubt as to the impact of James' inattention to those commitments. William was exceedingly blunt in his assessment of the negative effect James' decisions were having on him, his family, and James' son, John.

LETTER FOURTEEN

Dear Brother/

Long before the present time I trust you have had the pleasure of embracing your Loving Wife and Family and could I waft my wishes across the Atlantic I would say, may happiness by your Lot. If I could write contrary to my thoughts and act with dissimulation, you would not find such plainness of speaking as this Ler is likely to contain, and that I may not omit any thing I wish to write, I will as in a former Letter take the Subjects as I find them in my Book.

1st I have received only 2 Lres from you while some of your Friends have received 3 times as many. I do not know in what Light to consider this, having plausible reasons to conclude J. Brettargh has endeavoured to prejudice your mind against me - if he has done so, I frankly forgive him - I well know I am no favourite with him nor do I wish to be so

In Letter to Son John you say "In regard to Messrs Howarth's Coal Plans I left directions with Brother Wm how to correct them" and then add "had I them here I could make them right in 2 Hours." I acknowledge you gave me direction how to correct them, but not how to make them right. The directions you gave me I committed to paper - Mr. Albrisson & Knowles came to Worsley. I showed them the corrections you had instructed me to make, Mr. A. immediately exclaimed "this is no more than what your Brother & I tried for a Day together at Pendleton and could not possibly correct them so as to agree." I lent them the Plans considering that unless the Plans were corrected Messrs Howarth & Co. would pay no money. I have not got them back though I have twice called upon Mr. A. - In regard to your being able to correct the Plans I believe you are not, if you be, why did not you correct them while here as you had certainly 2 Hours to spare.

2nd Sale Club - My Sister would inform you the members of Sale Club are reduced to 9 in count and that these 9 have paid up all, or nearly so, of their Arrears & also subscribed the Deficiency to get possession of the Mortgage which they have now obtained, this has made some of the old members desirous to come in - Mr. Thornhill holds the Mortgage - Mr. Ratcliffe is not likely to live long he appears far advanced in a Consumption - I have paid 6 pounds toward your Arrears of Subscript there - At June 2 I was not there, being taken very poorly at Manchester abt. 2 Hours before the time I purposed to set out - I wish to know as soon as possible how your Shares are to be supported by me, having already paid on your act. upwards of 23 pounds more than I have recd. besides to our Mother

I have never yet seen R. Greaves nor have I any opportunity to call upon him, not having time to go to Manchester on my own Business - Mr. Clegg I called upon nearly every time I went to Manchester in the spring but got nothing - I am sure you will think it necessary to say something on the above when you consider I am abt. 5 pounds more out of Pocket than the Sum I have to receive on your account besides a continual outgo without anything coming in from you. Nephew John as I said in a former Letter shall not want while I have anything to bestow, but Clubs I am sick of - To Pendleton Club it appears you were indebted at the time of your Departure the sum of 31 pounds for Arrears of Rent & Subscription - Your Books as Exor I have not posted up but have made a resolution to do so in 28 Days from the Date hereof, if providence permit me to enjoy Health - Nothing yet done by the Exors they wont to spoken to for any Debt nor have I written to Mr. Horrocks for what you mention - the particulars I have quite forgot - but will see him if you will send me the particulars

now in regard to your Books as Exor if the other Exors get an order to Sell 'tis likely they will compel me to give up the Books - what is to be done relative to the Entries in them concerning Beet Bridge/ I have heard nothing from G. Hall since my last/ & other matters belonging to you, should not a copy be taken of them - An answer to these things you cannot return too speedily

I have written a Letter to Brother Thomas saying I cannot possibly continue to pay our Mother his share an longer, owing to having so much money to pay for the Club shares etc. and in my Letter, have stated what I consider an impartial Representation of you as Exor in the Capacity of borrowing money from him with reason for him not being paid again and your resolution of not allowing him to be a loser etc/ what answer he will return I cannot well say, to a former Lre he returned an uncivil answer

Our Mother I have paid her up to Apl last and then told her I could not pay her more than my own Share for the future - I have not seen her since Easter - Stephen was a Worsley on Whitfriday and said she daily grows worse. Stephen's Wife has done no work for 15 months past being very Lame, yet Stephen seems as Cheerful as ever - Sister Betty is very poorly she has got the Rheumatic Fever - Ellen is well - Mary is unwell her Arm gets no better - Matthew Halliwell & Wife are well. I have sent twice to request Matthew to write to you. - I do not know whether he has written or not.

The prices of Articles for Food etc. is greatly reduced. Flour, the very best 40 shillings. Bread Flour 34 shillings. (*Unreadable word*) the best 23 shillings or 24 shillings the Load. Cheese from 42 shillings to 50 shillings. The Potatoes New 1 pence 1 farthing the lb - Old Potatoes 5 shillings 6 pence the Load. Sugar such as was 10 pence when you left is now 8 pence the lb - Coffee and Tea are not reduced. Treacle is 4 pence the lb - The Labouring People are now much better off than the Farmers, who are sold up one after another all around. The Landlords will not lower their Rents and poor People will not pay more than 2 pence a Qt for New milk & 1 pence for Buttermilk & take little at that. Butter is now in the market 12 to 13 pence a lb at Manchester & 10 to 11 pence at Bottom though no good old Butter is yet arrived - Beef & Mutton are 7 1/2 pence a lb though Cattle are reduced 3 pounds a head - Fletcher of Booth's Hall hawks 1/2 of his Milk. Starkey of Worsley Hall leaves his at 7 Milk-houses and it is with difficulty they sell it. - E. Wenson of Worsley can only part with about 1/2 of his in the new; The rest he churns & hawks the Buttermilk & Butter also - Calamity is in the Farmer's Mouths. Mr. Bradshaw is not come down. I think he will have a warm reception from them

This Lre will come by one of Mr. Bancroft's Friends - My Wife and Daughter are well and join me in kind love to You and Family and we shall happy to hear that You are comfortable situated. I do not know whether John will write or not - poor Boy, he enjoys not good Health too much as your Departure preyed upon his Mind - I expect him at Worsely on Sunday next and will cheer him up as much as possible - Whatever may have been inferred from my Conduct etc. well know I stand but low on my Sister's estimation - I am with the strongest Affection Your loving Brother

Wm Stott

Worsley June 28: 1821

Letter Addressed to:

Mr. James Stott

White X Tavern in Philadelphia

More from England

No response to the above letter has been preserved. We have no knowledge of the effect of William's letter on James. The next correspondence in the Stott packet is a July 29, 1821 letter from son John to his parents. It is rich in detail concerning the Coronation of George IV and interesting reading from one who was a resident of England during those turbulent times.

LETTER FIFTEEN

begun July 29: 21

My Dear Parents/
Another month has elapsed since I last had the pleasure of writing to you. In my last I think I promised to note down weekly anything which was worthy of notice in the "Manchester Guardian", but this last month I have been deterr'd on acct. of my Master going to France soon after I sent my last letter to you (date the 27th Ult) which I hope you have recd. safe, together with a "Peep into Ilchster Bastille" & a lre from my Uncle Wm. per favor of Mr. Kinsey's son to your neighbour of that name, 'twas by the information of Mr. Bancroft I knew he was going. Mr. Bancroft left us to go to his Family in Wales on the 29th Ult - Good Man - worthy & affectionate Friend. In losing him I have lost the best supporter of my Courage and fortitude /Uncle excepted/ in the Absence of my dear Parents.

I have only seen Mr. Brettargh once since the departure of my dear Mother. /Augt 12/. Uncle and him were never

Friends since your departure to America and I have only been out twice since that time & when my Uncle asked leave for me to go out he gave me to understand that I had no occasion to go any where else (not that I think he wrote).

You may guess what has given me the most pleasure the last 6 weeks - 'twas the receiving your kind lre and that of my dear Sister, yours on the 7th July & dear Sister's on the 4th Augt. for which I return you many thanks. My Hand trembled as I broke the Seal of that of my dear Father's, and my legs failed when I read the first few lines of that affectionate epistle - I was in the Cellar and had not there been a cask beside me upon which I seated myself, I should have sunk to the Ground - I turned over the Sheet and on the last page the tender and affectionate names of Dear Mother - Brothers - & Sisters - met my Eyes - you may Imagine the change in my feelings for words cannot describe them - & I did not fail afterward to thank that God who has so kindly protected them over the tempestuous Ocean.

I was rather surprised to Read that Sister Frances was the Stoutest of any, She who here enjoyed so delicate a State of Health no doubt it will be much improved by the voyage - it depends entirely upon the State of the Body before they make Sail - I am not disappointed in my dear Father's Opinion respecting lovely Joseph - not a Word I think. I don't remember reading anything abt my sweet Chatter-Box. She has lisped her little Poems over many a time before now to her dear Father - not long ago I could have heard her - now I cannot. The thought brings tears into my Eyes - give her an affectionate embrace for me - aye them all a thousand.

I have the pleasure of reading Sister Frances' lre which Miss Ashworth recd. the day I recd. Sister Hannah's - I think Sister Hannah may not be offended that Frances has writ the best lre - perhaps Sister Hannah's head was not got clear - as Father has Informed me before that people's Heads are generally muddy a few weeks after they land and as sister Frances was not sick hers wanted no clearing - and I think the Wasps in the Sugar Pot was an idea of her Fathers, but they are both very well composed though the matter in them is not so much different.

I think you dont do much in the Public line if my Father can attend School regular - I hope your Crops have been to answer your expectations - We have had very few to call hot Days this Summer - the weather now /Augt. 21/ is the hottest we have had this season - in general Crops of anything have not answered the Farmers expectations here - in the Spring haygrass was so thick that they turned the Cows in to (*unreadable word*) as they said it could never ripen. So they could not have it both ends of the Year as I think they expected. Crops of Corn are very favourable and if the Weather continues as it is will be well got in and plentiful. The prices of Wheat etc. in London markets are as follows - fine Red Wheat 40 shillings to 46 shillings - fine Wheat 40 shillings to 42 shillings. Oats fine 20 shillings to 22 shillings. (*Unreadable word*). Flour fine per Sack 50 shillings 2nds 42 shillings to 44 shillings.

The Coronation as was expected took place in London on the 19th July - that is of George the 4th. His illustrious Consort our late most gracious Queen Caroline had no share in the gaudy pageantry of that day. He reveled in all the voluptuousness of Gaudy dress which the inventions of Man could make. The Queen did not let the time pass unnoticed for on the 17th July She sent a most dignified and spirited lre to his Majesty protesting & remonstrating against the recent decision and refusal of the privy Counsel to her request to partake of the Coronation, which she made on the 14th.

/Writ of the Augt. 24 1821/ On the Coronation day She

went in her Royal state Carriage to the Abbey, Alighted & sent her carriage away. She made 5 different attempts at 5 different doors to gain admission, they all said "we dont know you" though the Soldiers all presented Arms as she passed. At one entrance Lord Hood offered a ticket of admission for her but all would not do - they shut the door peremptorily in her face & she was forced to stand there till her Carriage could be fetched back.

Alas, Good Woman, She little thought She must change her thoughts of a Worldly Bubble for an Eternal Crown of Glory in a Kingdom of Bliss in less than 3 weeks from that time - Caroline our most gracious Queen left this World of Persecution and trouble on Tuesday the 7th of Augt. at 25 min. past 10 p.m. at Brandenburg House in Hammersmith which place at the time was a scene of the utmost Confusion, every man looking at his neighbour and with eyes uplifted "She is no More."

Dr. Lushington and Mr. Wilde together with 2 foreigners are her Executors - the Government contrary to their Will directed a person to remove the body on the Tuesday following. It was her will either to be interred with her daughter or removed to Brunswick, which last place was the pleasure of Government.

The person appointed to remove the Body had a Battalion of Horses appointed him which was quite against the feeling of the People & likewise orders which way to take it, which was through the Back Streets. Though the Rain fell in Torrents, yet the Assemblage of Respectable Persons all in Black even astonished the nearest Friends of the Queen and the press was so great as scarce to be able to proceed; when the people saw which they were going they immediately blocked the way up with Waggons, Coaches, etc. & forced them into the Public Streets. The Military fired upon them but their spirit was so undaunted (*in the margin*- 2 men were killed at Cumberland Gate) that when they attempted to turn again into the bye way they repeated their Design in spite of the Military. It was not a made up thing before because they all with one unanimous look, as it were, joined without speaking a word.

Mr. Brettargh called & Thursday the 23rd Augt. & told me was sending you some N.Papers & a lre by the Warren which ship I intend this to go by & I daresay you will see an acct. of it in some of them - it was not so on the Coronation Day. No, the Road and the Stands which they had erected were four fifths empty. They pulled down fronts of Houses etc., but they were not engaged & it is supported there was a loss to the owners of at least 40,000 pounds! So eager were the People to see the procession. Napoleon Bonaparte died on the 5th of May 1821 at S. Helena where he was Interred.

Note written along the margin of the first page
Mr. John Bellringer of the firm Russel & Bellringer & Co. died on Sat the 18th Augt. without a moment sickness

Note written along the margin of the third page
Uncle William is at this time very ill, worse he says than he has been for amany years back

Letter addressed to:
Mr. James Stott
New Jersey States
to be left at the Post Office Philadelphia
till Called for
North America

Directed to (*unreadable words*) to go by the "Warren" Augt. 28. 1821

My Country, Your Country

From some of his siblings and his father, John continued to learn about America as first experienced by the Stott family. Interestingly, James spoke of his native England as "your Country' when making comparisons in terms of taxes and freedom.

James did establish the school mentioned in previous correspondence and although attendance was less than he had hoped, the Stott children appeared to have benefitted.

LETTER SIXTEEN

Whitehorse Sept. 19 1821

Dear Brother John/

We received your Letter by Mr. Kinsey's son on Sunday the 9th instant who landed at Alexandria, in the state of Virginia, which City is on the left Bank of the Potomac about seven miles from the City of Washington where Mr. M. Corbett is.

We have several small Towns and villages around us. Haddonfield is a small Town about five miles from our house. The Glass Works at Clementon are two miles off; the owners have begun to blow window Glass; we have not been to see them yet.

We have had a great many pears this year, but not so very many Apples; September the 5th was a very rough day. It blow'd most of the Apples off the Trees, and blew two of them down; one of them was blown up by the root - the other was Broke off. A Mr. Inrat's Mill was washed down by the breaking of the dam; there was seven hundred bushels of grain lost.

My Father keeps school now, Brother James says very good lessons he spells little words and speaks up very well; Sister Hannah comes to school sometimes and is now got into Division; Maria learns Accounts she is in Multiplication; Eliza can write very well now on the slate and is very much improved in her reading and spelling; she can write figures and has almost learned numeration; and she is learning the Multiplication Table; I am nearly through Long Division.

We have had Water melons, Pomkins, Squashes, Mush melons and Cucumbers in abundance; we have Cucumbers lying dead on the ground. We have wild cherries here; they are very small and bitter things. People say they are very unhealthy; they make very good Vinegar; there are a kind of berries called Poke berries, they make Red Ink of them, they grow wild; there are both Chicken Grapes, and Fox Grapes grow wild in the woods, but I would rather have the Chicken Grapes; there are a many pretty flowers here growing wild that would be highly praised in Gentlemen's gardens with you; the Turncap Lilies grow wild here; the Huckleberries are all over, and now the Cranberries are ripe, but there is none about our house, but a many in Sion Meadows about seven miles off. I dare say we shall go some day to get some.

You will please to give our respects to Uncle and Aunt at Worsley and to our little Cousin Mary and to our Grandmother and to all our Aunts and Cousins at Middleton when you see them; and to all our old neighbours at Worsley, and to Mr. and Mrs. Brettargh and to their two Daughters; and to Miss Ashworths and tell them we are all in good Health, and when Apples are over we shall have plenty of Walnuts to crunch this winter.

You will please to give our love to all our Friends in Yorkshire, Aunt Lydia in Particular, and you will please to write to them as soon as you can. Sister Hannah is writing to Uncle William; You will please to give our love to Mrs. Mary Bancroft and her Daughters. John Bancroft was very well the last time we saw him; he has just been over to see his Uncle John below Wilmington, but is not come back; You will please to give my love to Miss Birches, particularly to Miss Ann. I wrote to Miss Ashworths when Sister Hannah wrote to you and have not yet received an answer.

I hope you have received the Letters safe, for my father says they are a week long; he means we are a week in writing them. Well while we are writing to you we fancy we are talking to you, so the longer we are writing and the more of your Company we have, but I must give over to give Sister Room to talk to you. She will have done in a Day or two so no more from your loving Sister

F A Stott.

Dear Brother John, When my Sisters did write to you before I could not write well enough, and now I cannot write as well as I love you, but I thought I would tell you that we have had such a sight of Cherries and Huckleberries, and Apples, and pears, and Walnuts (*unreadable word*) now wild Grapes are ripe, such large bunches; and (*unreadable word*) we have had more than enough of Cucumbers, and watermelons and pomkins such large ones, and Nutmegs, or Mush melons; these last are very sweet. Cows will eat all these things and horses too; and horses will eat Apples here, and so will Cows and Hens and pigs; our pigs live upon them and swill; apples sell now for 3 1/2 pence to 6 pence a Bushel and Cider for 4-6 shillings a Barrel; a great wind blew a deal of Apples off, and trees down too, about two weeks since, and now the Weather is so comfortable; the wind blew fences down too, and it rained so fast, but it does not rain so much here as it does at Pendleton, we have Apple Puddings, and Pies, and roasted Turkies and boiled chickens; and sometimes we say "I wish bother John had some of this pudding and some of this Turkey" because we love you so well; we are all in good health and love you better than we did before. I will write better the next time. I learn accounts; Sister Frances has written so much I have not Room to write more; or else we have such pretty Hens and Turkies; the hens have Puffs and muffs.

Maria Stott.

Love to brother John from little Eliza Stott

Dear Son John, your Sisters have all but filled this Sheet, no doubt you will be well pleased with their improvements in writing - they have all made rapid progress in their learning the few Weeks they have been at School. Eliza, it appears had been quite a Pet, she could read very little indeed, without great assistance - it appears Miss Mary had been in the habit of telling her the chief part of her lesson. She has a wonderful memory and makes great progress in her learning. I traced out the first part of the line above, but she writ her name without any assistance. Maria learns accounts very well and so do her Sisters - indeed I have plenty of Time with them; my school increases very slowly; Learning meets little Encouragement in my neighborhood - on some flimsy pretense or other they keep their children from school.

We expect to hear from you in a short time as the letter Mr. Thomas Kinsey brought was a long time in its passage; this comes with the first vessel which has sailed for Liverpool since his arrival here - he was swindled out of considerable property at Liverpool by Mr. Moony, the person to whom our friend J. Brettargh recommended him

Your Dear Mother and I frequently talk of you when you are asleep in Bed; as you generally go several hours before we do; though we are seldom out after ten o'clock. I should like to hear what has been the result of the inquiry into the abuses in Ilchester Goal; we have just heard of the Death of your Queen; and of the Insult offered to the people at her Funeral.

Give my best Respects to Mr. Goadsby and say I will be very thankful to him if he will let you go oftener to see your Uncle and Grandmother; I understand by William's letter that you have only been once in three months to see him; this Confinement say I humbly think is too close; it will surely be detrimental to your Health; I should like you go as often as convenient to see your Grandmother, and likewise your Uncle at Worsley; say I request him to let you, once a Month, go out as usual, such very close confinement as I understand you suffer, will most assuredly injure the Health of any young person - I say that your Life and Health are as much prized by your Mother and me, as his Son's Health is valued by him; he must, he does know, that a youth frequently requires an few Hours of relaxation; I do not wish him to grant you too many; 12 Hours in 28 Days, is only 22 1/7 Minutes per Day; one with another; I know you have too much good Sense to think this is any license to Disobedience.

(James' note continues along the left hand margins of the first, second, and third pages.)

I am sorry that the Spirit of Reform is weak at present in the Land - Cobbett is a shrewd man, it appears that the Boroughmongers must ultimately work their own ruin as that great Genius long since foretold - when the Army does not get so large a Share of the Spoils of the Poor, then it may grow discontented and join the Landed interest against the fundholders - but Belly band Reformers will do nothing. I wish the worthy Men who are now carcerated in jail may be provided for in a proper manner - do you ever hear anything of Mr. Harrison (the Parson) of

Stockport, he is in Chester Castle - in my next I will write you amany particulars which I have not room for in this. I will begin it in about 14 Days and finish it in time for the New York packet which sails the 10th of November.

Thank heaven we all enjoy good health; and are not troubled about Taxes- I have just paid the whole of mine for 12 Months amounting to about 7 shillings Sterling, for particulars of them see my letter to Mr. J. Brettargh - we have no Excise Officers here - Ale Cider and porter pay no Duty; nor malt nor Hops, nor any kind of Home made Spirits - the legislative expenses of this State including the pay of all officers, pensions, etc. etc. amounts Seventeen thousand Dollars ! a year. The whole amount would not pay four Lords of the Bedchamber in your Country - we can make shift to live in this Country without Lords; you will think this strange - whether it be owing to the temperament of the air or our Minds I leave you to Determine - Salt by the Bushel is a Cent per pound, it comes from England; happy people that can pay eight times the price you charge us - write often to us; direct to be left at the post office Philadelphia. Your Mother joins me in tender Love and Regard - take care of your Health - your affectionate Father James Stott.

Letter addressed to:
John Stott
at Mr. Goadsby's Chymist Druggist,
Chapel Street, Salford, Manchester

LETTER SEVENTEEN

White Horse Tavern Dec 3rd 1821

Dear Brother John,

I now intend to write you a Christmas letter, and Sisters Frances, and Maria are writing to Uncle William; we are all in good health at present (but Sister Frances has been sick of the Disentary) and I hope that you have enjoyed as good health as I have, for I never had better. We received a letter from W. Brettargh Dated August the 31st wherein he tells us that he sent a parcel of newspapers along with the letter but we have not yet received them though my Father has taken infinite pains to find them out.

Now Dear Brother I will tell you about the weather, it has been very much like an English Summer, but not so many wet days; on the 30th of Nov. we had Snow and it was very cold; we had a little Snow on the 1st of Dec. The 2nd was a dull day and began to rain heavily about 7 o'clock; 3rd and 4th were both fine days; 5th was a very wet day; 6 the ground was covered with an hoar frost and the roads very dirty; in October and the greatest part of November we had very fine weather; it was almost like spring; people say that this last Summer has not been near so hot as the Summer before was; we have but had two or three hot nights.

John Bancroft came over to our house on the 1st of Dec.; he has received a letter from his Father about a week back and is writing another to you in the parcel; he is working piece work at present but has got a bad cold; he wishes to be remembered to you and his Aunt and to all friends.

Brother James learns his lessons very well; he has given over spelling the words none, but reads them and speaks

117

loud (*unreadable word*); little Joseph is very fond of a book and a spade too to work with on the Road. Your Father had a great deal of trouble to make Eliza read her words correct; she had almost forgot how. Maria can read and write a great deal better than she could when she began to go to school, but my Father could not attend school for about a month, and that threw them back again. Now I will tell you how far we are got in Accounts. Maria is in multiplication, Frances in Reduction, & myself in long division, for Sister Frances goes to school oftener than I do; I cannot be spared to go regular; there is not much encouragement for a school here, people dont care whether their children learn anything or not; in this Country School Masters in general go round amongst the Neighbours, and get them to sign their name and put down as many Children as they intend to send.

In the first letter we received from you since we came here you wished to know whether we kept a milk or a cheese farm we keep only two Cows and two Horses and plough the most of our land. The Horses are now drawing Cord wood to the City (Philadelphia).

My Mother has lately been over to see Mr. N. Whitworth's family. Mrs. Whitworth is confined at present, she has got a Boy; they are all well in Health and appear to be pretty well settled; they live about two hundred yards over the Schuylkill bridge. My Mother says it is one of the finest bridges she ever saw; when you go on, it is like entering a house, it is rooft over like a barn and has sides and window to; all the Pennsylvania team drivers ride on the last Horse and their waggons have all Canvas covers.

Please to give our respects to Uncle and Aunt at Worsley also to Mr. and Mrs. Brettargh and to Mrs. Bancroft and family; you will please to call and give our respects to Mr. and Mrs. Livingston and Mrs. Hamilton and Conely and tell them we are well in health and like the Country we are in but could like to see our old friends sometimes; you will please to give our Love to all friends in Yorkshire when you write to them; also to all our Relations at Middleton Particular to Grand mother. My Mother wished me to ask you whether you have got your skates yet or no. I mentioned it to you in my first letter, but have had no answer.

They have a sort of Gigs here that will only hold one person which they call Sulky's; some of them have covers and some have not. We may buy silks here a great deal cheaper then we can in England. I could buy very handsome India silk Handkerchiefs for a dollar apiece. I intend to send you a couple the first opportunity.

You will please to give our best respects to Mr. and Mrs. Baker also to Mrs. Bowring and tell her that her Husband has been very sick of the fever and ague but is got better my Father and Mother has often wished him to write but he seems quite dilatory about it now.

Dear Brother I must conclude for I have not left my Father much room to write; we all join in respect to you and all Mr. Goadsby's family I am Dear Brother your ever loving Sister Hannah Stott

Dear Brother John, you are a great way off, I love you, and Miss Mary, and Miss Ashworth, and Sarah Brettargh, and Margaret, and Ann Birch, and Hannah, and Mary Crossley, and Margaret Slater, and a deal more; and my Uncle William, and aunt, and Grandmother, and all of them; James loves James Diggle, but I love you better than any a great deal; we have Custard now, and apple pie, and a sight of Pigs; I love you best I am sure; this is my Christmas Box; My Father says I grow fast, but I am your little Eliza yet; God bless you. John are you well?

Eliza Stott

Dear Son/ I am certain you will be proud of little Eliza's Writing; I assisted her a little in the first three lines and to the Word Grandmother in the fourth; all after is her production; the word John in the last line is excellent; I hope you are in good Health and Spirits and trust you got our October Letters safe; yours came safe to hand so did Mr. Brettargh's; I should have ansd. his before this, only I have been so puzzled to get the parcel he sent - I have done all I could to find it, and only got it a few Days since. I thank him heartily and will return him a long letter this approaching Xmas and another to you - if your hands are chipped this Fall as usual I advise that you wash them over Nights and Mornings with the liquid called Tanning used by Chymical Tanners if Mr. Goadsby thinks proper - perhaps you have a letter upon the Road for me, pray continue to send me all the News you can; your Information is pleasing to me - I will write to you again in ten Days and give you all the Information I can - pray take care of your Health - J. S.

P. S. You will have seen my letters to Mr. Brettargh of October last, which I began in July; we have the News here of G's visit to the Deer Land; are the People there grown mad? or was it only the venal part of them that shouted for hire? I have composed a Song[1] which your Sister will send you in the next letter - We have something in Papers here about Geo. seeing Caroline in a Vision while on a visit to the family Estate at H---r, that he shrieked out in all the Horrors of Despair - that with Difficulty he was appeased - that to hide his Valour, his Lords in waiting gave out that he had had a violent Twitch or pinch of the Gout - that he Trembled and Sweat three Hours; that during this period the Regent's punch had lost its usual effect upon him, etc. etc.

Trade is very very brisk here, at this Time - Twist[2] cannot be got into the market fast enough - - - I have nothing lately from Europe - I go but seldom to the city - and our Country Newspapers dont take much notice of Foreign News except something in the way of J (?)eer.

Learning meets with little encouragement in this part where I now am; a Preacher I heard on Sunday last said, in one part of his Sermon "that he verily believed that if a person was to come into this part of the Country with the whole Range (he meaned Circle) of the Sciences in one Hand and an Axe in the other, and bid them choose which they would have, their choice would be the Axe!" I agree with this preacher in this Matter

Your Mother enjoys particularly good Health and so do I; your Sisters have had much better health than I expected considering the green fruit they ate - Hannah thrives fast she is almost as tall as her Mother, Frances I believe is much troubled with the worms; I wish Mr. Goadsby would be kind enough to favour me with a recipe for them in her; Maria is healthy, works hard and learns well - Eliza is as hearty as she can be, as sharp as a Needle and active as a Girl can be; she has made wonderful progress in her learning since I opened School. James is healthy, works hard, thrives fast, and learns pretty well. Joe is flower of the flock; he is active with both Hands and feet, but cannot talk - his Mother indulges too much - he has the breast yet - give our joint Love and Respects to all our Relatives and friends you must not forget Mr. Brettargh - the (*unreadable words*). Your Christmas Box will follow this in ten or fourteen Days. J.S. Love to Mr. ad Mrs. Goadsby and to Thomas.

Note written along the bottom of the fourth page
Always Direct for me "to be left at the Post Office Philadelphia till called for." and tell Mr. B. to do the same. A merry xmas to you - and happy new year - take care of your Health

Letter addressed to:
Mr. John Stott
at Mr. Goadsby's Chymist & Druggist
Chapel Street, Salford
Manchester

[1]*The song to which James referred is probably that which appears at the conclusion of Chaper VI.*

[2]*"Twist" presumably refers to the twisted silk threads used for making button holes, etc.*

Dissatisfaction

James acknowledged that he and many of his English neighbors had become increasingly disenchanted with Gloucester Township. Not only was the farm and tavern proving to be less and less appealing, but his school lacked sufficient students to make it profitable. Though close to Philadelphia by today's standards, the Township was far enough in 1822 to be decidedly rural. Its inhabitants were characterized by James as being, for the most part, uneducated, and classroom instruction for their children was not a priority. With those factors in mind, James made the decision to close his school and instruct his own children at home. His plan was to move his family to Philadelphia within the year.

Discontentment was a feeling with which son John was also dealing. When John wrote to his father complaining about the difficulties in his apprenticeship under Mr. Goadsby, James' advice was clear and concise, "directly speak your Grievances and ask for Redress" while remaining "docile and obedient." As stated by James, "I paid money for you to learn a Profession," not to become "his hired man."

LETTER EIGHTEEN

White Horse Tavern March 10 1822

My Dear and beloved Son/

We received your very affectionate and rather too despondent letter of December about a month ago and ten Days since we got the letters and present from Mr. Goadsby which it appears were brought to Mr. John Sharp by some person from the old Country, and have been in his Hands but a short time - please to give my kindest thanks to your Master for the Book. Say I have read 64 pages of it; the Subject is pleasing to me, but had Mr. Hindmarsh stated the argument of Mr. Pike (if he used any) and confuted him it would have yielded me more pleasure. Mr. H. only states Mr. Pike's assertions, shews his extracts from the Baron's writing to be garbled, and offers a few of his own observations; together with contests, etc., etc. I am aware of the Difficulties in answering such Works as those of Mr. P. and think the whole Works of the enlightened Scribe ought to be read and compared with a cool head, a head panting for good and Truth, and a mind not fore judiced, but open to scriptural convictions; for, like the divine Word, if taken in parts, to natural Reason, they may appear strange, mysterious, contrary etc. etc., but viewed as a whole they will appear in their proper light.

In the part where I at present reside, the natives evince no love of good; they love whiskey best, (and were I disposed to serve them, I could sell more on the Sabbath then in the other six Days) they value not learning; few comparatively speaking being able to write more than their own name; they may be divided into four Classes or Sects, viz. Quakers (or Hickory Quakers), (*unreadable word*),

Methodists, and men whose Minds may be compared to a Wilderness; I am pretty persuaded now that I have need of time to learn and know more of the Country; that I could not have placed myself down anywhere so (*unreadable words*), so Ignorant and wicked a Part as where I am.

I told you that I have several English neighbours who are all Sick of the Township we are in and fully determined to leave it. Mr. Kinsey offers his Plantation for Sale and is very anxious to dispose of it. Mr. Jones has sold a part of his and will soon dispose of the Remainder. I took out another license yesterday, but do not expect to Stop here another year. I will remove into the Neighbourhood of the City - direct for me thus: "J. Stott White horse Tavern, N. J. to lay at the Post Office Philadelphia till called for." You need write only N. J. for New Jersey, or N. Y. for New York.

We all of us enjoy remarkably good Health excepting Frances, and she's much better than usual - tho she is yet puffed and swelled - she must be plagued with the worms - Jem is a brave fellow, quite healthy and strong; he is particularly fond of his brother Joseph who is a most winning little fellow; he thrives like a young Cedar, learns to talk surprisingly, Sucks his pas, beats his mother, and calls himself Joe Joe; Eliza shoots up quickly, is most uncommon sharp and sensible, learns fast, she can Read, spell, and write better than any girls in the state of N.J. of her height and weight - Maria is much the same as usual; she learns well, is the best worker we have, and cannot possibly have better health. Frances as above, learns her Book, likes to act as Mrs., direct her Sisters, but loves little work herself. Hannah is tall and comely, Industrious and useful, learns well, and we all love her.

Our dear Son John - we hope he is in good Health by this - the Reading of his last letter brought Tears adown our cheeks. But my dear Boy keep up your Spirits, be not humbled over much to man - raise not, nor encourage a Spirit of Opposition; let cool reason, two or three times digested form your Resolves; and then nothing should cause you to recede - always remembering that no Resolve should be contrary to the divine ordinances, nor against the laws and right Customs of your Country. Get your Uncle to wait upon Mr. Tindall and copy the binding part of your Indentures, and the teaching part (which belongs to Mr. Goadsby). I did not bind you to Son Thomas, neither are you bound to your Master's family; only by the laws of decency and respect, which laws are reciprocal - nevertheless be you docile and obedient, as cool reason points out, but again I say, be not humbled over much; rather live a freeman than a Slave - look round, see how other apprentices are generally treated. I paid money for you to learn a Profession, not to be a Boots nor a Scullion; and if I would fancy you could demean yourself so much as to submit to such drudgery, I certainly should advise you to the Contrary, I had almost said disown you; are you not Mr. G's Apprentice? not his hired man. He pays you no wages, I paid him to instruct you, does he perform his part? if not, see and require that he do it. Remember you are made of the same materials as Mr. G. Be not daunted, be not cast down.

Be not afraid, call up courage and modestly, manfully, and directly speak your Grievances and ask for Redress - Wait for your Master's answer and be sure not to interrupt him in reply - wait coolly and respectfully he has done speaking and be sure not to answer pertly and when he speaks to you, pause a few seconds after he has done before you begin to reply - of all things avoid complaining without a just Cause, let not small things trouble you, do not shed Tears when you speak, that shows anger and weakness - it is most unmanly (*unreadable words*).

If your Master's Son offers you any the least Indignity, spurn it, but first of all let him know that you intend to do so. Sometime when your mind feels free and easy, address to the following effect, "Thomas, I have for time past borne your taunts and jeers, your insults and proudly given orders with as much calmness as I could; first because you are my Master's Son, who I respect; and secondly, because you are a little funny fellow whose fierce anger has no other effect than to raise a smile of Pity; and thirdly considering you are the Lord of the kitchen and the parlor fires, I thought you might forget yourself, and sometimes strive to lord it over me, but now I wish you to remember that you are your father's apprentice, and rather younger bound than I am; learn to conduct yourself as becomes a younger apprentice, for I am determined to take your insults no longer etc. etc."

I gave up my school on Friday, having only about 21 scholars at most, besides your Sisters and Brother James, who I intend to instruct at Home; your sister Hannah is for teaching a few girls I understand, but am afraid it will not answer. I have not received one Cent of school wages since I first began. Money is not over plentiful and those that have it are very loath to part with it - they will make (*unreadable word*) hundred excuses before they will part with one Dollar - they will offer Corn, Rye, Pork, Hay etc. at about 12 to 25 per cent dearer than it is in the Market and a many actions are brought forward in this Township for as (*unreadable words*) Quarter Dollar.

The Inhabitants are a mixture from all nations, English, Scotch, Irish, Welsh, (*unreadable word*) French, German, Swiss etc. and these again combined in endless variety, but they all love Liberty. I agree with them in this - here is all the Liberty a Man could wish for. The high Sheriff of our County called in this Friday Evening to take a glass of Brandy toddy; he fastened his Horse and Gig to the sign post, and sat down in the House chatting freely with the Company, a part of whom he knew, and let them drink of his glass; at his Departure he wanted no Ostler[1].

The head judges of our Court are equally free and affable. The whole Sum granted by the house of Assembly for the Expenses of the State (during the last Session) for the ensuing year was Ten thousand Dollars; this is the whole amount allowed to the Governor, the Supreme Judges, the Members of Council and House of Assembly, and the Armory; for keeping the Government House in repair etc. etc. ! What do you think of this?

Now a hired man in the farming line will have from 8 to 13 Dollars per Month and found; in my humble opinion the working Class here are the most independent men in the world; they have nothing to fear if God grants them health - in the winter Season they go out with their Dogs and Gun, as freely as an MP can in England; they Hunt the Rabbit, the Raccoon, the Fox etc. and shoot partridge, Pheasants, wild Ducks, Deer, Bears etc. The owners of the plantations do not many of them like working - those who do, prosper and get on in the world - those who do not, first mortgage, then sell their Lands and work or go back into the western Countries and purchase Land there.

I purchased about 11 1/2 acres of woodland lying two miles from my House which I am cutting down and drawing home. You would say it was very wrong in your Country if your Neighbors cut down fine thriving young Oaks no thicker than your leg for firewood; but so it is here. I have had five or six men at once cutting it down (chopping they call it here). I purchased it only for work for my Horses. The wood will about pay for wood and land and all I expect; so that I shall have the land clear - it has no fence around it and is worth no more when the wood is off then two Dollars per acre! The price was $8.31 per acre. This to you appears very cheap, but John, advise your Country men when they

come here to take Poor Richard's advice, "At a great
pennyworth pause awhile." I bought wood the last Fall
and during the Winter have drawn it down to the River just
opposite the City - during the Frost, I drew it over the Ice
on Sledges and sold it, but found it hardly to pay.

Mr. Whitworth wishes me to go near to him and keep
School, but that is what I do not like; Children are kept in
no order at Home - all Liberty mad - of course they cannot
be kept in order at School. I have some thoughts of getting
onto a Canal at present, if I can; but your Uncle has kept
all my rough plans, else I wd. have finished one or two as
a specimen.

In your Uncle's last letter he mentioned what sums I
have recd. from the Commissioners of Road, but omitted
amany which he will find all together

on one page in a small Book - he has not enter'd what
I paid for Brick making Coal etc. at Salemoor, and a great
many other Disbursements; I know I am from 250 to 300
Pounds out of pocket, but do not expect that I am any
more. The reason I did not write sooner in answer to him
and you is that our port has been frozen up and no Ships
could possibly go down the River; a beautiful Ship called
the Dido in attempting to go down the River just when the
frost set in before Christmas, was jammed fast in the Ice
and sunk. She was loaded with Cornmeal and India Corn,
bound to Liverpool - she is now got up and is in port to be
repaired.

I take in a weekly paper - the following is an extract
from this Day's, "The papers from England were never
known so barren - all appears set still and Silent. John Bull
lies upon his Oars; the affairs of Brother Paddy do not
seem to bother him." "Alexander acts with great Caution
and Mystery; the Germans are smoking their pipes except
about 30000 who are watching over the Slumbering
Neapolitans. The Spaniards are stabbing each other as the

occasion may require. The French are boisterous and violent as usual - John Bull is quiet but keeping a sharp look out to see what all these Things are coming to, for he never likes to see any fighting unless he has a Hand in it."

I thank you kindly for the information you have sent me, and I hope my dear Son will continue to favour me with (*unreadable word*) way; and now the Ice is gone he may expect to hear from me as usual though I have nothing interesting to write about excepting his dear Sisters and Brothers.

We are going to have an Election for a new President of the United States; and four candidates are already named. It is expected the contest will be Sharp and Keen - Manufacturing goes well; Domestic goods meet chief demands. Ashton Barlow is weaving his own and I believe it answers well.

Hope in my next I shall be able to tell you we are doing the same; (*unreadable words*) my School through the Winter Quarter. I have not yet begun as I mentioned in my last but one. Though the winter (*unreadable words*) good weather in general; excepting a few bad Days it has been passably fine, almost always (*unreadable word*) underfoot - have not the least Cough upon me neither have I have during the frosty weather.

Now my Son John I have thought proper, in consequence of what my Enemies were endeavoring to do, to make over to you all my property in England of all kinds and descriptions, hoping you will have the Goodness to divide it proportionally with your Sisters, but this is at your own discretion. The Indenture is dated March 3. 1822 and signed before an Alderman of the City and has a Notary Public's Seal to it, testifying that said Alderman is what he purports to be; now some Persons tell me it is necessary to have it signed by the British Consul here, and others say it is not; but I will shortly make proper inquiry and upon satisfying myself that it is complete will transmit it to you; I hope you will make proper use of the property when you are in possession of the Deeds, and not run wild and squander it away; in my next letter I will write you all Particulars I remember concerning the Clubs and such other matter as I conceive will be useful to you and your dear Uncle in managing the Business in all Respects.

Your dear Mother has been very unhappy since the rect. of your last letter. She as often burst into Tears when she has thought of your forlorn Situation (as she calls it). Lame and almost friendless, few if any calling to see you; and not able to walk out if you had Liberty; nor at Liberty to speak what you thought under the Ear of your Master and his Sons when your friends did call; your Sisters have likewise felt keenly for you; they all send their kindest love and respects to you and hope you will be perfectly restored to Health before the receipt of this - we frequently gaze upon your portrait which is hung upon our best Room and Sighing, walk away; but Dear Son we have no need of a Picture to remind us of you; your image is so deeply engraven in our Hearts that time and distance will never obliterate it; distress not your tender feelings with such Frances; imagine not that we forget you; even little Joe is taught to lisp your name, and can point out among the Pictures, "Buddy John." Give our kindest and best Respects to Mr. Brettargh. I am certain he does not rec. all our letters; he has never told us whether Mr. Knowles recd. my letter of July or Augt. last, full of Sketches Sections etc. We all desire to be most kindly remembered to him and Mrs. K., to son Robt. and all the Family; if Mr. K. has not received the above mentioned lre., I will direct no more to him for I am certain if I do he must not have them; but will direct to Mr. Brettargh with a K on the top left hand corner. Hannah is writing to Miss A. Williamson, Frances has written to the Misses Brettargh.

Your Sisters all desire to Subscribe their name to this as a token of their Love and Respects to an absent Brother, absent in Body, but present in the Spirit - your Mother sometimes Dreams about you, but not often as she could wish. Hannah saw you a few Nights since in her Slumbers, but had little Conversation, for somehow you was taken away - in your last you said nothing about your friends in Yorkshire; please to give our Respects to them, and say something of them when you write to us again, you must not forget us to your dear old Grandmother etc. etc. at Middleton.

Hannah Stott, Frances Ann Stott, Maria Stott, Eliza Stott

Pray do not cross your next letter with Red Ink, except it be of a better sort than that you crossed the last with, it was quite puzzling and bad to read, as the Red Ink spread and run into the Black. Your Mother says she would rather have two letters than one crammed so, but we are quite thankful for your endeavours to oblige us.

During the winter I have been very busy, foddering Cows and feeding Hogs three times a Day till we killed them off beginning of February - I had my School to attend to besides - we killed nine and Salted up eight of them for our own use.

We wish all of us to be kindly remembered to your Uncle and Aunt at Worsley; he may expect a letter when you receive this - your Mother does not like me sending word that Joseph sucks yet - you would laugh to see them sometimes, when they are quarreling, but dear Son I will bid you adieu - my fingers ache - this letter contains from three to four thousand words - you must give our Respects to Mr. Brettargh's family, to Mrs. Hamilton & Daughter, to Mr. Livingston and family, to Mr. & Mrs. Baker - your kind friend J. Bancroft will meet this letter on the Ocean - his son John has written to you lately, I believe.

Remember us to Mrs. Bowring and family, to James Diggle etc., to the Misses Ashworth etc. and all friends and acquaintances; we have not seen Mr.. Bowring since Augt. - he has been sick we understand - perhaps he does not take care of himself - we do not know - give our Respects to Mr. Goadsby & Mrs., to your Uncle Stephen and Aunts at Middleton, to Mrs. Brookes and Alice etc. etc.

We pray God to keep you in Health and preserve you in the pure spirit of Good & Truth; -despond not. John Bancroft sends his love to you. We will say no more at present, than that we shall always be your loving Parents
    J. & H. Stott. March 20.1822
    This is my Birth Day. Aged 44 J.S.

Letter addressed to:
Mr. John Stott at Mr. F. Goadsby's Chymist & Druggist Chapel St., Salford, Manchester.

[1]*The word "ostler" is probably a variation of "hostler," meaning a groom or person who takes care of horses at an inn or stable.*

Looms in the House

Philadelphia had 104 warping mills employing about forty-five hundred weavers by the year 1830 (Gordon [a] 386). According to James, in 1822 there were many weavers working out of their homes, finding it to be a profitable occupation. From this next letter, we learn that James purchased two looms with the expectation that Hannah would begin earning some money as a weaver; Hannah's reaction was less than enthusiastic. For his part, James again stated that he had begun to tire of life as a farmer in rural New Jersey. Clearly, the

Stotts were becoming anxious to return to some semblance of the type of lifestyle they had once enjoyed in England.

LETTER NINETEEN

My dear Son John/

I was at Philadelphia yesterday, saw Mr. M. Corbett, who Sails from N. York shortly with his Daughter I suppose, tho' I had not many words with him, as I am going to see him in the morning; I thought I would again write you a few lines, and send them by him, though you will scarcely have had time to read my long letter which came by N. Y. and your Sister's to the Misses Brettargh and Williamson of Foster's Wood.

I have nothing new to send you, only that we have got our pair of Looms Home and are starting them next week; it seems to hurt your Mother's pride to have Looms in the House, but she is rather better reconciled to them since hearing and knowing that our Esquire's Ladies are some of them Weavers and can and do earn about as much with weaving as their Husbands do with letting out Law or Justice.

This is the finest Country in the World for working peoples; Husbands men and Mechanics are more independent than their Employers at present, though Trade goes remarkably well, and both cotton and woollen Goods are in great Demand at present; our Domestic Trade increases rapidly. Mr. N. Whitworth informs me he has received a letter from his Brother who tells him cotton Goods and provisions are exceeding low with you and that we expect, of Course, to be inundated with your manufactured waste, but we begin to prefer our good Cotton to your feed, and believe it would pay John Bull the best to send us the best of his Twist from 30 to fifties (in the pound). In a very few years we shall not want that.

I met with an old weaver in my Neighbourhood this morning as I returned from measuring, or running the lines as it is called here, of a plantation; he complains that weaving is not so good as it used to be; he can only get 12 1/2 Cents per yard for weaving Domestic or homespun 9/8 wide and 36 picks in an Inch - he shot a glancing Arrow that English weavers had brought down prices - amany of my neighbouring weavers, for I find upon inquiry, that there are no fewer than a Dozen within a Circle of Six miles round me, weave with the Hand, as weavers used to do when your Grandfather was a Boy. In Philadelphia and just round the City there is now Forty thousand yards of cotton Goods woven weekly. A very few years back I am told there was not more than two thousand per week manufactured.

I called upon a weaver near the City one morning last week and found him at Breakfast with his Family, Tea and Toast and two sorts of rich Cakes and roasted oysters adorned his Table; he invited to sit down and partake with him; I stood no Ceremonies seeing such luxurious fare - he comes from near Bolton, and lives about 1 1/2 Mile or near 2 Miles from Market Street. The old weaver I talked with this morning was riding his Horse; he keeps a Gig, for the old woman and hisself (I always thought himself wrong).

Englishmen often hurt themselves when here by excessive drinking Spirits etc. and so low - else they might do uncommon well.

The Deeds of Property which I mentioned to you in my last, I am informed are correct, and have sent them to you by Mr. M. Corbett, who I doubt not will deliver them safe; and I hope you will watch well your rights and be not intimidated by words from whatever Quarter they come; or by whatever mouth they are uttered. Sale Club I expect will more than clear itself by this, and in a few years, if you will look at the articles you will see, it will make a

Handsome Sum.

We hope you are quite recovered of your lameness and are in good spirits; be not discouraged if you do not hear from us so often; sometimes Ships are a long time in coming over; The Feby. (1st) Packet from Liverpool to N. Y. is not yet arrived and the Lancaster that sailed before that is not yet come in and has not been heard of since seen on the Banks of N.foundland. It is said she is bringing Twist for Mr. Thos. Grundy. We sometimes miss the Ship we intend to write by and sometimes we are put off by something or other; but however the thing is in that respect we never forget you - no, no - we never forget John; even little Joe can call on Buddy John.

Farming is good to nothing where I live. I will give it up after this year and go nearer to the City, into Pennsylvania; it is expensive crossing the River and, too, a journey. Your Mother was there yesterday and on account of having Looms to bring and a many Errands, it was nine P.M. when we got Home. To Day I have written a Deed or Lease of the Premises which I Measd. this morning, so that I am most tired of Scribbling and it is now near to 10 P. M.

Oh! I had like to have forgot to tell you that your Mother is sending you a Silk Handkerchief by Mr. Corbett, your Sister F. A. made it and Hannah marked it. I hope you will receive it safe, and John, mind you do not wipe the Tears off with it; perhaps they might take the Colour out.[a]

We all of us enjoy remarkably good Health except F. A. Pray send me the Receipt for the gravel (?) which J. (*unreadable name*) Esquire was so kind as to give me; it would have been of service to me several times since I landed if I had had it. I left it in the Book of Physic in Black print. I wish Brother William had sent me a few more of my Waste plans - they might have been of some use to me.

Pray remember us to Mr. and Mrs. Knowles & Robt.,

to Mrs. Mr. Brettargh, but he will have my letter before you can receive this; You will always remember us to your Grandmother and uncles and aunts; we often talk about them.

I like this Country much better than England, but I do not like new friends as well as I like old ones. I am too old to seek new acquaintances. The manners of the People here are different to the manners of the People in England; and do not think they are a little honester here than they are with (*unreadable word*).

In your next give me all the local news you can and tell dear friend Brettargh to do the same. I am afraid he has not received two of my letters, or else he is making me wait as I did them after the arrival of my family - Brother Stephen nor Matthew Halliwell never writes to me. Thomas Matthews of Stakehill I hear is got married at Stubenville. I stopped all night at an English Tavern in the City and while asleep some villain stole my money - it was not much, but it was more than they had any right to - this was last week.

> We all desire our love to you and Friends
> Farewell.
> James Stott.
> My last I wrote on my birth Day the 20th Instant and
> we did not forget you on your birth Day.
> Evening past 10. March 30. 1822

Note written along the left margin of the third page
I have just read this letter over to your Mother, and seen several Errors which I hope you will nullify. Your dear Mother & Sisters request to know who the Miss Bennett is you mention in your last letter and desire their respect in return.

[a]*James' footnote concerning a handkerchief*

Your Mother bought you two; but she does not like one of them; she will send you anon by Mr. E. Grundy who is expecting to return sometime this Summer. she will buy the best she can next time; now she had no choice; no time, but she knows you will like it because she has sent it; oh John, how she loves you; your letter made her and Sister H. cry.

Letter addressed to:
John Stott
at Mr. F. Goadsby's, Chymist & Druggist, Chapel St.
Salford,
Manchester

Chapter VI
Committed

Severing the Ties

The remaining transatlantic letters, spanning the year from April 1822 to May 1823, speak to the fact that James had emotionally as well as physically committed himself and the family to the immigrant American experience. Persuaded that reform was not forthcoming in his native "land of Tyranny and oppression" and convinced that he could never tolerate the policies presently in place, James began the task of shaping the parameters of a new life.

To that end, James discussed the termination of his English business ventures, the disposition of his property, and the settling of any outstanding accounts. While acknowledging his longing to return to a transformed England he could once again love, the bulk of his writing was focused on his adopted country and the problems and accomplishments of his wife, Hannah, Frances, Maria, Eliza, James, Joseph and himself.

LETTER TWENTY

White Horse Tavern April 29th 1822

My dear Son John/
Your very affectionate and welcome letters came to hand yesterday, two of them by the vessel from Liverpool to N. Y. of the 1st Instant. They arrived at N. Y. in 23 Days. I thank you very very kindly for the intelligence they contain - were it not for the Information I receive from you and from my respected friend Mr. N. Whitworth I should be almost lost in a wilderness, for barren would it be in every sense of the word, were it not that I receive so much information by your Epistles.

On the 20th of March I writ to you a long letter, but I have little to send that can be much gratifying to you - it was my birth Day; I am glad you remembered it. On the 24th we toasted an absent and beloved Son, wished him Health and Spirits, and many happy returns of the Day.

On the 30th I writ to you again by favour of Mr. M. Corbett who is returning with one Daughter to the Land of Tyranny and Oppression; by him I sent you a good and legal Title to all the Landed Property and Houses I possessed in England - do not be afraid my Dear Boy; borrow money upon Sale Moor property and buy yourself clothing and pay for your washing yourself. You will see by the Deed I have taken the power out of your Uncle's hand and given it to you - now I have only to beg you will use it at discretion, with discretion; and as property is diminishing so fast on Value perhaps it would be as well to sell it if a favourable opportunity offered; I told you it was mortgaged for 230 pounds. The Title Deed was at Altringham but now is in the hands of the Sale Moor Club, or "New Chester building Society."

You can now either let your Uncle continue to manage, or give the power to some one else; but consider, it your uncle has faults about the Business, he has, I dare venture to affirm, one great beauty, he is honest. I writ to him by the Packet Ship from N. York in March; and gave him my opinion concerning large and material Sums he has omitted entering on the both Dt. and (*unreadable word*) Side of the account; indeed had he sent me Copies of the accounts by your Dear Mother as I wished for, I could long ago have balanced and returned them or had he sent them now by Mr. Bancroft, they would have been returned in about four months at farthest.

I think I forgot to tell him to send My Settlement (to Samuel Horrox) between Mr. John Barnes of Tenter and the Exors of C. Hill, relative to Eltonfold bleaching works. His lease is expired a year ago, and I know that Settlement is correct as far as it goes, and that no other person or persons can bring it right, because they are not in possession of the Documents I was; and if they were they could not understand them.

I am sorry he has not got the money from Mr. Tindall in regard to Mr. Clegg. I told him before that John Brookes could prove the work was done; he should have sued him as I desired in the Court of Requests, in Manchester.

I cannot hear from my good friends Mr. A. Knowles - I have sent two letters to our very respected friend Mr. J. B. of Pendleton since I heard from him - I believe I get most of his letters, they give me great and to me valuable Information, tho' it appears he does not get above one half the answers; I have perhaps seasoned them too highly; Lord Sidmouth's circular[1] empowering every puppy in Post Office to stop suspected letters, has suspended their nearer approach to Pendleton; tell him to continue writing to me and I will do the same to him. I perhaps sometimes will be able to find him.

My last to him was chiefly loaded with American Politics, including what we know of the young Liberty Sprig in Columbia (South America) which our Congress has acknowledged to be properly planted, and sent out an accredited Minister to assist in watering and watching. I made up the freight with observations upon your government, some of whose Agents have hearts as hypocritically white as the Chalk Cliffs of Salsbury Plain.

John Bancroft Jun. has written to you (again) by Mr. Corbett - he is well and has just received a letter from his father (I understood) stating that he intended Sailing on or about the 18th Instant by (was it) the Tuscarora. I shall feel happy to see him, tho' upon the whole I dont know how the country will suit him; nothing in the farming way, I am certain, but what I mentioned in former letters will answer; except he had a very large Capital, and would go a Distance from the City, say 70 to 100 miles and take or purchase a grazing Plantation upon a large Scale and sell his well fed oxen at Philadelphia or N. York.

The primest Beef is now 12 1/2 Cents peer pound for Ribs and Surloins, other prices of same Ox, from 4 1/2 to 10 Cents. Mutton very low. Butter high - Pork some as when I last mentioned it - wheat 1.25$ per Bushel of 60 lb., wheat flour 7.00$ per Barrel, Rye flour 4.25$. Grain is up at present. I dont know why?

We increase Manufacturing every Day - Any Man with a working Family may live very well here - as to a Man with a ladylike family, and small means, the Lord have Mercy on him - tho' he do not need to fear the Tax gatherer, he may fear the Silks and Laces in the City; they are so bewitchingly beautiful.

Lawyers, Doctors, Physicians, Mathematicians, Philosophers, painters, poets, etc including the whole Race of Learned Professors had better stay in Europe than come hither; if a man be learned, he need not shew it; he may work and hold in his Philosophy if he pleases.

Spring is "progressing" as the noble Marquis would say, rapidly here; Cherries are larger than peas, peaches are knit and thriving fast; some kinds of Apples are the same, other kinds not yet fully out of Blossom. Peas are in Bloom, Rye is shot, or in other words shews itself in the Ear. The woods look beautiful- such a diversity of Colours, from the half opened Bud, to the full spread leaf - the wild flowers are springing and beautifully expanding; we have little music in the woods. The Robin cheers us a little, not much; and the "Whippur-will" tells us his name from Setting Sun, until Midnight - in the Morning he repeats his Song "Whippur-will" - his note is rather sharp and shrill, much unlike that of your "Cuckoo". The Frogs are the best whistlers at this Season of the year.

John Bancroft is now over to see me and will take this letter for Mr. E. Grundy to deliver you; or perhaps Mr. James Wadsworth will bring it to you; he is a very affable, intelligent, and kind hearted young man, and can and will, if you see him, tell you amany things - he is disgusted with the "Affected Learning" of this Country. He has not travelled much here, but he can describe the City to you pretty well; I mean that part of it which he has seen.

He came over to start my Looms. Your Mother appears rather more reconciled to our weaving since the Dollars come in by it, than she was at first; and tho' I told her Esquire Thackery's Lady (wife, I mean) was a Weaver she could scarcely credit it, till the Esquire called one Day to see me weave with a double Boxed fly, which is quite a curiosity here; and it chance he had a Reed in his Hand. Your Mother thought proper to inquire of him if his Wife was Weaver or did weaving; he answered in the affirmative; it pleased her, and then she told him, that she could weave as well or better than I could. I have woven from three to four hundred yards of Gingham, and am now getting Geers for Domestic which; I propose weaving at ten Cents per yard. It is 5 Quarters wide, and has thirty four picks in an inch (sometimes not more than 28). My neighbors have 12 1/2 Cents per yard for the same, but they pick it with the hand as your Great-Great-Grandfather did; by weaving it lower than the others do. It is expected we shall have more than we can do. Please to ask friend Brettargh what sort of wage he thinks it will be?

I was at the City yesterday, and your Mother was along with me; it is a treat to her almost to see the City, she goes so seldom - we saw several Persons from Yorkshire, particularly a Man and his Wife that know your Aunt Lydia and family very well; they are wool Dressers and are doing very well. Your Mother wants to live nearer the City, and I now think it would be better for us, as we are too far from Market; so, it please God we live, we intend to Remove next March, or sooner, if we can make things convenient.

I herewith send you a copy of the Song I composed last November, indeed it was not composed; it was written extempore.

When at the City yesterday, we heard that the Ship which takes our friends to Slavery Island was sailing a few Days sooner than we expected, so that I have not time to write all the letters I thought to have sent, neither have your Sisters the opportunity which they to embrace of writing to you; you will please to excuse them and they promise to write by first chance they have in future. We are all well in Health and hope you are the same - continue to write as usual - your letters are great comforts to us. Love to all friends - tell them we often think of you all.

Your Mother weeps when she sees your letters.

J.S.

Note written along the left hand margin of the third page
Your Mother sends you the other Handkerchief she promised you,

in the last letter which you will receive by Mr. Corbett. She also sends by this same conveyance a ten Cent piece, a five penny bit (Spanish Money)=6 1/4 Cents, a Quarter Dollar or 25 Cents, and a half Dollar or 50 Cent piece, all of Silver on purpose that you may see our Coinage; rec. also a few Cents of Copper by the Bearer and a small Sketch of the White Horse Tavern, our present Residence. See the cap of Liberty on the Head of our American Money.

The letter itself contained no address. Presumably it was sent in a packet with other items such as the handkerchief from Hannah, the sketch of Whitehorse Tavern, and the samples of United States Coinage.

[1]It was Lord Sidmouth who, in reaction to the escalating reform demonstrations, introduced the Habeas Corpus Suspension Act in the House of Lords on February 24, 1817. The Act was passed by a vote of 150 to 35 and was ratified by the House of Commons on March 1st. (Halevy 23). Despite the Act, pressure for reform continued, prompting Lord Sidmouth to issue a circular to the Lords-Lieutenant of the various counties experiencing demonstrations. That circular, mentioned by Stott, called upon the Lords to adopt any measure needed to maintain order. Further angering the Reformers, Lord Sidmouth wrote a letter congratulating the local authorities on the actions of the yeomanry during the infamous Manchester Meeting (Halevy 63-64).

Based on James' experience with English governmental intervention measures, it is not surprising that he suspected his often radical letters could have been intercepted.

LETTER TWENTY-ONE

White Horse Tavern, Gloucester County N.J. Sep. 8. 1822

Dear Son John/

We have been waiting, since the last of June, in daily Expectation of a letter from you; your mother has been deeply affected at Times on account of not hearing from you; I have endeavoured to comfort her with the Story, of "Ship so and so, being hourly expected at Philadelphia," but within these few Weeks so many Vessels have arrived from Liverpool and no letter from you, nor from any Friend, that I cannot have peace any longer without writing; we expect that you have had two or three letters from us since we heard from you. Our letter by Mr. James Wadsworth would be recd. from his Hand with a small Token of affection from your Mother; and we expect Mr. Corbett would favour you at or about the same Time with a more valuable Present. Though we can thus send you, at the Distance of four thousand miles, these tokens of our Love and Esteem, we find it impossible to express in words the mental expressions of our affections; but trust you will believe that whether you write or not, we shall always remember you; your not writing causes us to think of you too much.

This has been a Sickly Season in this Quarter of the world, at New York the Yellow Fever marches at the Head of the Grim Tyrant's troop; he is greatly dreaded, in so much that the Inhabitants fly in various Directions; a many of the wealthy merchants and principal Hotels, are removed to a Village called Greenwich, about two miles out of the city, near to the Hudson or North River; at Philadelphia, Dysentery and Intermittent Fevers are commanding for the Fleshless Despot, and though not half so Dreaded as Yellow Fever, they sweep as many to the Dust hole as he does in the same space of time.[a]

In the Country, the Dysentery and ague have been very prevalent, the former kills a few, the latter destroys none. Son John, I believe that if you were in this world you would not be surprised at Disease being so prevalent; in June Children begin to pull unripe fruit that grows wild then they eat Cucumbers instead of Greens or Potatoes to all kinds of meat - Breakfast Dinner and Supper presents a large Dish of them - Cold boiled Pork and Cucumbers and Bread is the Chief Diet morning & night of the Labouring Class of this Season; and in the latter part of June, all July and part of Augt. - in July and Augt. they eat very plentifully of mush mellons, cantilopes & water melons; occasionally boiled Pumpkins are eaten with their pork - also they eat apples pears Turnips etc. and drink very plentifully of cold water.

The middle of the Day is hot; the evenings and mornings sometimes are very cool; they wear light clothing in mid-day; of course in Evenings they wear the same; Oh! how chilly they are; then they swallow whiskey by Gills to warm them; and pour cold water by pints after it to cool the burning Spirit. The women and Girls (as well as Men and Boys) in the Country go without shoes and stockings - the hot Sands at mid-day almost burn their feet - at night & morning the Cold Dews chill them.

Your Mother and Sisters (except Frances) and Brothers have followed the Customs of the Country pretty much though not altogether, this summer; and some of them have felt the effects of it; your Mother has had the ague three times; but she is well at present; Frances has had it two times, and so has her Brother Jem; they are both completely recovered of it at this time; all the rest of them have escaped Sickness in general; and we are all in very good

Health at present, except Frances, who is much the same as usual; she has taken the medicine you prescribed without good effect; her Belly continues very large, and in her features she appears more than commonly Sick considering that she goes about; her Mother now fears that she is dropsical, and talks to her about Death and Dying, but the poor Girl keeps her spirits up wonderfully, though she often complains of a bad appetite.

Your Sisters are all gone, at present to see Thomas Kinsey Jun. and family; they live about eight miles from us, through a small place called Blackwood town; we expect them at home again this Evening; they have taken my Horses and Market waggon with them.

Your Brother Joseph is famous little fellow now (he has weaned himself) and he talks wonderfully; I know you would enjoy his prattle very much; he fears nothing, he has a noble and dauntless Countenance. Jem's face is not come to itself since the ague, but he is quite healthy and works hard. Eliza grows now and does not chatter half so much as she used to do; we have called her chatter box till she seldom speaks in my presence. Maria is our Milk maid; she is healthy, has rosy Cheeks and queer temper; she grows apace, gets up in a morning, cuts pumpkin for the Cows, Milks etc. Frances is as above stated. Hannah is healthy, tall and slender, likes her Bed in a morning, works very well sometimes, but I think she is not so good tempered as she was - she is rather too contradictory; I do not like that Spirit - pray you avoid it, and tell her to leave it if possible.

I have not seen Mr. J. Bancroft this three months, but heard of him last week.; he has four looms at Work, and is doing very well, and all his family's in good health; Mr. Whitworth has four looms going; he and family are in good health; we had two of his Sons over on a Shooting frolic Monday & Tuesday last; they returned on Wednesday.

The oldest is a very keen Sportsman- he killed 6 brace of partridge on Tuesday.

James Barnes, brother to Lambert Barnes, the Fiddler, is dead about a month back - he met his Death by Intemperance - he lived in Hamilton Village not far from Mr. Whitworth (leave word at the Ship Inn that his Brother may hear of it). Several English Men are dead in the space of Six weeks back; when I go to the City I generally hear of one or more having paid the Debt of nature - indeed we are numerous now in and about the City.

If you see Mr. Wadsworth you may tell him his other has but a Sickly house, two of them have the Ague and one or two recovering; is it not wonderful that People here will Shake five or six weeks, when they can, if they will, be cured in one Day? The last we heard of Mr. Josh. Walker of Baltimore he and part of Family were sick; Mr. Sidebotham (who married Kate) is in a good Situation.

Cotton and woollen Trades are both very brisk here and wages pretty good - in a few weeks an active person that never wove before, will earn three or four Dollars per week; a regular weaver will earn from 6 to 8 or 9 Dollars per week. Machine Makers (for Spinning, Carding, etc.) have two to three Dollars per Day and are much wanted in these Part.

Crops are pretty well in this Country this Season; part of my Rye was good and part middling; my potatoes are in a good Crop; and Corn looks very promising; peaches are plentiful; they have sold from six to twelve Cents per Peck in the City, and now the finest the pick of the Market are not more than 12 1/2 Cents or 6 3/4 pence per Peck - Apples are wonderfully plentiful; in the Country fine fruit will not fetch more than 6 3/4 pence per Bushel - I have just sent 40 Bushels to the Cider Press, and have all along fed my Pigs and Hogs with apples (I have 5 Hogs & 6 Pigs). We have cut and dried in the Sun some of our Pears, and wish we had dried apples (*unreadable word*) do good as they are. Markets here are much the same as when I last wrote you. (*Unreadable word*) Beef and Mutton which are always low in the Summer (we bot. Salt Beef yesterday at 3 Cents per lb.).

The owners of the white horse property are about selling it, and we intend to remove into the City or neighbourhood (in Pennsylvania) the next Spring, if not sooner; I expect your Sisters will write to you as soon as we receive your next letter; they have been very busy lately or you might have heard, read, their prattle before now.

In your last letter you never mentioned my Dear Mother and Brother Stephen & Sisters (why does not Stephen write to us); give our Kind love to them all, and say we request a letter from them. Mr. Brettargh has not written this long long time; I have aimed two letters at him since I received his last - give our love to him and family - and give our Respects to all friends at Pendleton and Foster's wood - what does James Williamson think of things now. When you write into Yorkshire give our kind love to all friends and Relations and say we should be very glad to hear from them and all friends at Middleton; do remember us to, when you go over.

In your answer be sure to give us all Country News that you can - tell us all that you think will be interesting to us upon all Subjects and Cases; our Elections are coming on here, but there is no bustle, no hurry, no canvassing about them - all still as at other times - I shall shortly give the first vote I ever did give for a Legistlator - I am pleased with he privilege - I feel proud of it - how different from the Alien Bills in Europe is this?

I will send you some old Newspapers and extracts when I send Mr. Brettargh a Stalk or two Corn. I will put them in a Box; he should let me know who to direct it to at Liverpool. We all join in wishing you Health and happiness

- in four weeks I will write again - yours affectionately
J. Stott.
Sep. 8. 1822

Note written along the margin of the third page
Your Uncle William will hear from us at the same time you rec. this - hope they are all well - William Bowring is in health - he is a perambulating Butcher - that is, he travels with Mutton in a wheelbarrow - your Mother sends her love to his wife. All your Sisters greet you with a loving Kiss - little Joe points to the Chimney piece and says "Buddy zjon dere." "dats tuddy Buddy zjohn."

Along the left hand margin of the first page James inserted this footnote
[a]From 3 to 7 die of yellow fever per Day in N.Y. - last week 32 died of yellow fever and about 50 of other Disorders making a total of abt. 82 in Philadelphia. 78 died in the same time before yellow fever set in - at N. Y. they buried from 75 to 80 each week - from which you may see that yellow fever is more dreaded than it is dreadful.

Letter addressed to:
Mr. John Stott, at Mr. Goadsby's
Chymist & Druggist, Chapel Street,
Salford
Manchester
Sep.8.1822

by the first Vessel from Philadelphia to Liverpool.

LETTER TWENTY-TWO

Philadelphia Nov. 17th 1822

Dear Son John/
I embrace the present opportunity of sending a few lines to you by Samuel Wardle who is from Bradford in Yorkshire; he says he shall stop a Day or two with his Sister in Manchester and will deliver this Letter safe into your Hands.

Since my last writing to you we have had a very sickly time of it in our family; the Ague and fever has pulled us all down very much; your Sister Maria is the only one of the family that has stood it out; she is quite healthy, and has been so during the whole of this Sickly Season, and the oldest men living can never remember the Country so sick before, as it has been this fall; we are with the Blessing of Providence fast recovering, as we never shake after taking a certain powder which I get, until we have caught a cold, but the least cold will bring it upon us again; amany of our neighbours have shaked from six weeks to two months, while we have been sick and well several times in that space of time.

The young man this comes by is sailing with the Ship Tuscarora for this port to Liverpool, and he brings a small Box[a] for Mr. John Brettargh containing eight heads of Corn, and three Stalks with the Heads, Leaves, Tassels (tops) etc. on them, cut into two lengths and numbered in such a manner as to enable him to put them together and see how they grow - indeed, if he will follow the Directions I send along with them he may grow Corn himself; perhaps he cannot get it ripe. (The above Corn I grew upon my Farm, from which he may judge of the produce of the Sandy Jerseys).

Paper No. 1 contains some Extracts cut from Newspapers etc.; as mentioned on it, this Parcel or paper is for you. No. 2 contains acorns, Hickory nuts and walnuts (two sorts); No. 3 Raddish Seed; No. 4 Pumpkin Seed; No 5. Castor oil Beans; No. 6. mush melon or Nutmeg Seed; No. 7 water melon Seed; No. 8, Calibash Seed; with directions for planting etc. all of them - I sincerely wish they may all come safe to hand; that he may plant them, and that they may prosper; and that he may live in Health and happiness until the acorns become large Oaks, and the hickory and walnuts as much in Girth as Mrs. B. now is, or ever was.

I do not know that I have any News that can be gratifying to you at present, as I have and heard little since I last wrote to you; your last letter and that from Mr. Brettargh I recd. together about six weeks since; in Respect to the Death of the noble Marquis, I think the government will feel his Loss, perhaps Mr. Canning is as fit a person to succeed, as his Majesty could have selected; is the new Marriage act any better understood than it was? Are amany Licenses taken out for the sale of Ale, Beer etc. in consequence of the late Law?

I thank you kindly for your last Letter, it was received with great pleasure. Your Mother thought she had lost her Son - we just removed into the City but not yet fixed - I will write again as soon as we have settled and answer your Queries as to the Sale Moor Club etc. - I have not written to your Uncle these three months or more; he never answered my last Letter. We trust and hope he is well. We kindly thank Mr. Brettargh and Mr. A. Knowles for their friendly offer in his last Letter. I should have sent Mr. K. some specimens of this Country Coal but the Box was fast nailed before I left the Jerseys, perhaps I may have another opportunity.

Mr. Thomas Kinsey Sen. has sold his plantation of 197

acres for about 2350 Dollars Cash and 809 acres of Land in Pike County, 400 acres of which lies in its wild state near to the Delaware River about 100 miles above this City, and the other 409 at such a Distance that he was told he could not go to it and return the same Day - that he would have to sleep in the woods as that Quarter of the County is totally unsettled; he did not chuse to sleep in the woods at this cold Season, and of course returned without seeing his Land.

Mr. N. Whitworth is laid up with St. Anthony's fire - all else well - I have not seen Mr. Bancroft this long time - understood he was well - Mr. Thos. Grundy is getting better - Mr. Francis Wrigley and family are well - we all join in kind and loving Respects to you and all friends - the Messenger is waiting -

adieu adieu
James Stott

ªThe Box is about 3 foot long, 11 1/2 Inches broad and 8 Inches deep, of rough Boards, nailed together in the same homely manner that Soap or Candle Boxes are.

Letter addressed to:
Mr. John Stott at Mr. F. Goadsby's Chymist & Druggist,
Chapel Street, Salford, Mancester

Problems at Home and Abroad

It was in November of 1822 that James and his family moved from New Jersey to Hamilton Village in Pennsylvania. Tired of farming and suffering from chills and fever, the Stotts appeared relieved to be living in a less rural area. Hamilton Village, in Philadelphia County, was slightly more than a mile from the permanent bridge over the Schuylkill River. Although the village was small, having only a couple of east and west streets crossed by several others running north and south, it was its proximity to the city of Philadelphia that made it attractive to the Stotts and others. In fact, by 1830 the village had from 50 to 70 dwellings (Gordon [a] 190-191).

James' next correspondence focused on his own personal difficulties both in America and in England. Politically, he remained concerned with the progress of reform in his native land, requesting information about current conditions in Manchester and Parliamentry proceedings. James mentioned the Presidential campaign in the United States only in passing. About the elections he stated, "I take little notice of these things - I do not feel much attached to American Politics."

In fact, the 1824 election to which he professed little interest was one with a noteworthy outcome. Five men, all Republicans, John Quincy Adams, Andrew Jackson, Henry Clay, John C. Calhoun, and William H. Crawford, decided to run for the Presidency. A wildly opposed Congressional caucus (attended by only 66 of the 216 Republican representatives) chose Crawford. The other candidates ignored the caucus and went directly to the people using state conventions as a show of support. At the Pennsylvania nominating convention, Calhoun agreed to a Vice-presidential slot (Dangerfield 310-311). In the national election, the final votes of the electoral college were 99 for Jackson, 84 for Adams, 41 for Crawford, and 37 for Clay (Dangerfield 336). With no one receiving a majority, the slate went to the House of Representatives. Although Jackson had received the most electoral votes, it was Adams who was victorious in the House. Clay, having advised his supporters in the House to vote for Adams, was henceforth suspected of making a corrupt alliance in order that he be appointed Secretary of State (Dangerfield 339-441). James Stott's reaction to the election was never recorded.

James did comment on the political problems in Europe. Indeed, Southern Europe had become a hotbed of revolutionary activity much the same as had been experienced in France. The governments of both Spain and Naples had been toppled by those with reformist goals. Becoming alarmed at the rapid spread of these revolutions, Metternich of Austria had drawn up a document at a meeting in Troppau in 1820 advocating the protection of recognized European governments by an international force. Neither the French nor the British agreed to sign and Lord Castlereagh of Great Britain urged Metternich to send his own army to any place he feared might threaten Austrian interests. After Russia and Prussia agreed to join Austria in endorsing the Troppau protocol, Metternich invaded Naples. The revolutionaries either fled, many to Spain, or were killed and Ferdinand I was restored as King. The King of Spain was himself engulfed in a battle to regain power at home while also attemping to maintain control of his Spanish colonies.

In an attempt to stave off more widespread insurrection, the Congress of Verona was convened in 1822. Spain and her colonies were of primary concern, and the major powers proposed an international mediation between the two. To that idea, however, the British voiced strong objection. George Canning who had succeeded Castlereagh as foreign minister, stated that they had "called the New World into existence to redress the balance of the Old" and was completely opposed to any action which could threaten the colonial trading advantage enjoyed by the British. Without at least the neutrality of the powerful British fleet, no international force could freely sail to the Americas. Thus the plan for international intervention was abandoned. Canning was desirous of the United States and Great Britain releasing a document showing diplomatic solidarity, but President Monroe had other intentions. He independently issued a statement that became known as the Monroe Doctrine, essentially affirming the concept that revolutions in the Americas were not the business of European nations.

The war between France and Spain to which James made reference was the result of the next action of the Congress of Verona. The French proposed that they dispatch an army to Spain in an attempt to quell the revolution there. When the Congress of Verona agreed, France sent 200,000 men across the Pyrenees in 1823. Eventually, meeting with little opposition from the populace, Spain's King Ferdinand VII was restored to his throne (Palmer 449-452).

LETTER TWENTY-THREE

Hamilton Village. Feby.22.1823

Dear Son John/
Your kind, intelligent, and affectionate letter begun Sept. 22 and ended Nov. 4. 1822, came safe to kind with the Newspapers etc. on New Years Eve; it was very gladly received I can assure; we were then sat musing and almost chilled with cold in a small cottage in this Village, but your Letter warmed us all; I had suffered with the Chill and Fever all Day, when Mr. N. Whitworth sent up the Parcel from Mr. John Sharp - both N. W. and I are at a loss to know the Reason why our friends do not write to us oftener - we fancy our letters are stopped on the way. Your last is full of interesting information and we thank you very affectionately for it - we earnestly request you to write regularly to us whether you receive letters in ans. or not.

We have deferred writing to you since our letter of Nov. last which we sent by a young man going to Bradford in Yorkshire along with a Box to Mr. John Brettargh containing 1. Extracts from Newspapers etc. for you. 2. Hickory nuts, walnuts, & acorns. 3. Raddish Seed. 4. Pumpkin Seed. 5. Castor Oil Beans. 6. Mushmelon Seed, three stalks of Corn with the heads on and foliage, besides eight Heads of Corn. 7. Water Melon Seed. 8. Calibash Seed, which things I shall be happy to hear that he received safe.

I say we have deferred writing writing on account of being out of Business; it would have been more than two hundred Dollars in our way if we had stopped in the Jerseys until spring, for since the Time we removed (in Nov.) until the 1st. Instant we have done nothing but expend our money, and have also had a great deal of Sickness in the Family which has helped it to go faster than it otherwise would have done; the man who purchased the White horse Tavern and also agreed for my farming Stock, left the Country abruptly, saying he was going to England and would return in March; we cannot hear anything about him at present; if he does return I shall have an action against him for Damages; I have the said Tavern still upon my Hands, the first owners not being willing to take it from me.

The last season was remarkably sickly, chiefly Fever and Ague, of so uncommon a kind as to baffle the skill of our best Physicians; amany Persons lingered from July or Augt. untill Christmas; I began in Sept. and never was well above a few Days together till the middle of Jany.; during the few Days I considered myself well by appetite was voracious, and I suppose overloading my stomach increased increased the Bile so as to bring on the Disorder again; for in my humble opinion it arises almost always from a Disordered state of the stomach. I suppose that I was attacked more than a Dozen times and took medicine; the last time the Shaking changed into Chills of a few minutes duration, which Chills returned about each 10 or 15 minutes for two Hours; after that a much Slighter Fever than usual for about three Hours; in a few Days the Chills came only once in about 20 or 30 minutes and were over as soon as an electric Shock; and then Fever and all left me; but I assure you I was left in a poor and debilitated State.

Your Dear Mother suffered severely; so did your Brothers and Sisters, except Maria; she is rough as possible and always healthy; they all got well before me; you would have been sorry to have seen poor Joe. When the fit was approaching, the Cherries left his Cheeks and the Rubies his Lips; the little fellow would pull his Mother by the apron and say with a tremulous voice "Mammy me going to chill again." Thank God we are all well at present, except Frances; she, poor Girl, is very bad; we are going to take her to a Doctor Eberle in the City, as soon as the weather permits.

It is now snowing very fast and did so all Day yesterday; it lies about a foot deep on the level; it is the first Snow of any consequence we have had this Winter; and it will soon waste away as the Sun is now powerful in this Country. We have had a few Cold Days but not many this Winter; indeed none colder than I have felt in England, though upon the whole it has been an uncomfortable Season.

Both the Cotton and woollen Trades are dull here at present, owing to the great influx of Brittish Goods the last Summer and Autumn, which were sold at public Vendue (or auction) for Cash at, perhaps, three fourths of the prime cost in England! Then there would be Carriage Brokage, insurance & Commission to Deduct here so that I apprehend the Merchant (who shipped) would not get one half of first Cost in his Returns. The poor Spinners, weavers etc. in England must feel for this! Here we expect a Change for the better in a few weeks.

We have had no arrivals in our port since about the new year, at which Time we were amused with extracts from the London, Liverpool, and Paris Newspapers indicative of War between France and Spain; well, let it be so; the nations of Europe cannot fight fair for six months, unless John Bull lends a Hand, but supposing the Ministers lend a Hand, will the Clodhoppers, and the People (who boast themselves "The source of Legitimate power") join them? The Clodhoppers cannot, according to our accounts; and surely the "Source of Legitimate power" has, by dear bought experience, learned better things.

I was very happy to hear that my old Friend Isaac

Ashton (Timperley) was in the Land of the living; I confess that I have often thought he was gone "to that Bourne from whence no Traveller returns." I hope you have let his dear father and mother know how to direct to him.

In respect to Sale Club, I shall like to have the accounts D. and Cr. between the Club and me fairly stated. I do not think Mr. Johnson qualified to draw out a just account; your uncle William wants experience (and I believe he does not seek for it) - get an Article (I have not one) see when the Chief Rents became due, and compare the Measurements etc. Remember the Club must pay for all the Land it has built upon and fenced in, what is in front of the Houses, the Streets etc. and for all the Land trespassed upon etc. for the whole time occupied.[a]

How can your Uncle think the Exors of Cha. Hill have a right to the Chief Rent, except he is willing to think every thing against me, have the Exors paid off the money due at Altringham; have they paid off the Debts due by the late C. Hill, or have they paid any part of them or have they proved by any means they had not assets to pay them? Your Uncle has certainly lost his Charity; if not, he has lost what judgment he had upon such things; see by the Club Books what money or Rent (*unreadable word*) Club has received for the extra House I bought of Mr. Lomas (of the Angel) or how that Rent is disposed of - if they do not give you Credit for all the Rent, you ought to appoint a person as agent and receive it yourself.

I do not think it necessary for you to commune with your Uncle about this Business as his knowledge does not extend to such Concerns. I request him to send me Copies of my a/cs. and I would fairly adjust and return them say nine or twelve months- ago, and my Character have been cleared of Obliguy. I am anxious it should be so; but perhaps it is the Self Interest of loving Brother to Keep me an Excile for ever; I cannot, I will not think such a thing of them, but why does one talk, and another act, as they have done?

We are now keeping the Green Tree Tavern in Hamilton Village one mile from the Scuylkill or permanent Bridge, in a direct line with Market Street in the City of Philadelphia, indeed it is called Market Street where we live; the Situation is high, dry and very pleasant; we all like the place remarkably well, and fancy or guess we can do well of Business.

As we have not Room to name one half of our Relations and friends, be pleased to give our kind Love and respects to all of them without exception particularly your Grandmother at Middleton and all your Uncles Aunts and Cousins in all places and Directions. In your next give us some account of Trade, Cotton, woollen etc., the farming Business, the Parliamentary proceedings, the King (God spare him) and all other things concerng. the Town and neighbourhood of Manchester (your letter to J. B. was highly pleasg. to Mr. Whitworth who saw it). J. B. desires his Love to you - he is going with his parents to a small woollen mill near Wilmington (on the Brandywine) - it is thought by judges in the Business they will do well there. I wish they may - we saw them well about 4 weeks ago.

Our Newspapers are all now filled with Matter concerning the election of our next president; there are several Candidates for the office, Crawford and Adams (at least their friends) appear to be confident of Success - I take little notice of these things - I do not feel much attached to American Politics - England! I love thee and were thy Sons and Daughters as free as the Children of America, thou shouldest be my last Mother. Amany English have return to England from this City during the last six months - amany of them worthless people - they have Roast Beef and pudding; for Skilly-ga-lee and potatoes stewed stewed in their own fat.

160

I should like to hear from my dear friend J. Brettargh and am hourly expecting a letter, giving an account of the safe arrival of the Box, Corn, Seeds, etc. which I sent him - hoping you are well.

We remain your affectionate parents. H. & J. S.

Dear Brother John, We thank you very kindly for those presents you sent up by Mr. Bancroft. Sister Frances is very sick she has got the worms you must excuse us for not writing to you but we thought we would let alone till we got fixed somewhere we live at a very pretty place now in Hamilton Village we have several boarders three of them Englishmen lately come over. I like the Book you made a present of when we sailed I have read it over and over again it is so entertaining Frances's is a very pretty book too. I will tell you more when I write again we are all well except Frances at present and hope you are so too. I am your very loving Sister Hannah Stott. Frances A. Stott.

ª The Chief Rents commenced you will remember from the time the Houses were let on prospect to be built. Your Dear Mother and Sister wish you to give their love to Mrs. Hamilton and Daughter - the name of the Place where we live reminds us of them frequently.

Note written along the left hand margin of the first page
I saw a very singular Vision in the Jerseys, last Tuesday Evening, just after Sun Set, as I returned to the white horse after being out in Search of money - the Phantoms were not disagreeable, but the fourth time they appeared in great numbers, forty at once - one of them spoke to me - I left the road, they beset me so - and they appeared again to me in the field.

Note written along the left hand margin of the second page
Send me a few Newspapers printed since Parliament met - I suppose they are now at their works of Deception on the feelings of

the Nation - how is Mr. Henry Hunt - we live about 1/2 mile from Mr. Whitworth - he and family are well.

Letter addressed to:
Mr. John Stott, at Mr. Goadsby's,
Chymist and Druggist
Chapel St., Salford, Manchester

To go with the 1st. Vessel from Philadelphia to Liverpool

From the Last Mail Packets

The final two letters were an exchange between James, the children in America, and son John. Shortly thereafter John, too, emigrated to the United States to begin working as a druggist, thus ending the flow of Stott correspondence crisscrossing the Atlantic Ocean.

LETTER TWENTY-FOUR

Hamilton Village, April 1, 1823

Dear Brother John/
I thought I would take this opportunity of writing you a few lines which I can send to Manchester by a young man who is coming over to Oldham to fetch his wife but now I am begun I cannot tell what to write about, only people here dont think it much to cross the Atlantic and come back again - it only takes a few months. I should never mind coming to see you and returning here again after seeing and talking with my dear Relations and

Schoolmates. I wonder why they do not write to me; I should like you to call upon the Misses Ashworth, and give my best and kindest Respects to them, also my Sister's; tell them we should be happy to receive a Letter from their Hands; give our very best Respects to Miss Ann Birch, & her sister, Hannah, and to Miss Marg. and to Sarah Brettargh, and all our School mates; I wonder they dont write to me; they might write if they could persuade theirselves to begin.

I should write oftener to you but I cannot start, but when I have started I cannot tell when to stop, for things keep coming into my mind faster by half than I can write them down, and while I am writing one thing, I forget another; but I will not forget to tell you that I am now in good health and spirits and so are all of us, and we live in a very pleasant Village on high ground, above the River Schuylkill, just one mile from the Bridge; we can see a great part of the fine dull City of Philadelphia; I must leave Room for my Sisters to write or else I would tell you a deal of things; I will send you some trifling Present, I dont know what yet, but something that you can look at and say "Sister Frances sent this," but tho I can send you a present, I cannot tell you Dear Brother, how well I love you,

F. A. Stott

Dear Brother John

As my Sister Frances has begun I will follow her in writing to you; you know she is older than I am, but I am taller than she is; besides I am always healthy and strong, and she is often Sick. Sister Hannah is almost as fat as John Bull used to be, and not quite six foot high; Eliza is very well she is little, and very sharp, she goes to School; Jem is a rough Lad with a face like a harvest moon, my father says, but I think the moon has a rounder face than

he has; Joe is a very sharp Boy and looks very well; he is quite master of all but my Father; he can chop wood, and crack a whip, and talk, you would laugh to see, and hear him; you must be sure to give my kind Love to uncles and aunts, and my dear Grandmother at Middleton, and to Uncle William particularly; and to the Misses Ashworth and all my old School mates at Pendleton and Worsley, Sister Eliza must write, so I will conclude your loving Sister
    Maria Stott

Dear John,
Now Frances and Maria have written. I will try to write a few Lines, to tell you that we all are very well, and that we love you better than we did; and that we shall be so glad to see you again one day; James is almost as big as I am, and he is such a rough Boy, he does not smoke Segars yet, but amany Boys do. I am very dear Brother John, your most
    Affectionate Sister
    Eliza Stott

April 2. 1823
My Dearest Brother/
It is with the greatest pleasure I embrace this favourable opportunity of transmitting a few lines to you hoping they will arrive safe and find you very well in health as they leave us all at present Thank God for it; Sister Maria had no cause to tell you about me being lusty for I assure you she is thriving like a fine Orange shoot and looks well in proportion; Sister Frances picks up a little now, and though she is small in body she is great and old fashioned in Spirit; I have not time to write many lines as I am going to assist in the washing of our clothes; give my Love to the Misses Williamson of Foster's wood, and to all friends and

Schoolmates mentioned by my Sister. We know nothing of M. Bowring; he left Philadelphia some time ago; we had very rough weather on Easter Sunday, but now it is charming fine; accept of all our prayers, and best wishes, for your welfare; we did not forget you on your birth day; my Mother made some mulled ale, and we drank your Health and wished you amany happy returns of the day. Father wonders he does not receive a letter form you, and from Mr. Brettargh, he has wrote to both of you since february. The Ship Dido sails tomorrow. Dear and loving Brother adieu

Hannah Stott.

Note written along the left margin of Hannah's portion of the letter

It is exactly two years to day since we had the Pleasure of seeing you last time before we left.

Dear Son, owing to the severe winds we have had no late arrivals from England, amany are on Tip toe to hear the King's Speech, and speaking generally, the People of this Country are very anxious for a war in Europe; we have strong Rumours afloat daily - the people here almost long for John Bull to put his foot into the war balance - they inveigh bitterly against him at present for taking possession of the Island of Cuba, which you know belongs to Spain - tho' it is not yet authenticated that he has done so. America has taken the Floridas from the (*unreadable word*), why should they be angry with John, if he does take Cuba? because they well know John's generous disposition; they know he will return Cuba at the end of the War if he do not want to keep it.

In my last I mentioned all the Particulars about our family, and have since been afraid it might make you unhappy, but dear Son grieve not - we are all well again; I believe you are right in what you say of the Cause of our Sickness; we eat too much Stone fruit last Summer and too much animal food - your dear Mother has got into quite another method of Cooking - she is too much in the Yanky way now - this morning the children had Beer posset[1] to Breakfast, and the Boarders and we had cooked Sausage, fryed hung Beef and ham and Eggs and Cold roast Beef, Tea, Coffee, etc. etc. on our Table - we did not live so, when in England - and meat three times a Day does not sit easy upon my Stomach.

I am in daily expectation of a letter from you now; I have answered your last about six weeks ago and sent to Mr. J. B. anor. letter about three weeks back by the Ship Alexander. Trade is improving here very fast at present. Mr. Whitworth and family are well. John Bancroft is removed to the Brandywine near Wilmington. F. Wrigley knows not what to do; he is now down in Delaware State looking at a Mill seat with John Wood. I will send Mr. Brettargh some Flower seeds this fall, adieu J. S/.

Note written along the margin next to James' portion of the letter
We are all in pretty good health at present. I wish we may never be worse, but I am doubtful - we live too highly - April 2. 1823

At the bottom of the first page there is the following from James
P.S. there is a regular Line of Packet Ships now established between Philadelphia and Liverpool; besure to send your letter by one of them. Their names are "the Dido - the Manchester - the Plato - and the Philadelphia" - one of the said Ships sails from this port the 5th Day of each month - and of course one of them will sail from Liverpool each month - it would be better if the Times of Sailing were advertised in the Manchester Newspaper - besides the above there is anor.

Line of Packet Ships from this Port to Liverpool and back again - the Alexander etc etc so that now we may almost write to each other any Day - when I came to Philadelphia this morning the Dido was dropping down the River and the Gentleman on Board that should have brot. you this letter - of course your Sister's present (a Handkerchief) does not come this time. I will endeavour to send it by the next vessel which sails, I think the 20th Inst.

This is Thursday Apl. 3.1823

Letter addressed to:
Mr. John Stott,
at Mr. Goadsbys, Chymist and Druggist
Chapel Street
Salford
Manchester

[1]*"Posset" is a hot drink made of milk curdled with ale, wine, etc. and is most often spiced.*

LETTER TWENTY-FIVE

Salford, Manch.
May 15th 1823

My very, Dear Sisters/

Your dear and affectionate letter came safe to Hand this Afternoon per favor of Mr. Jackson who lives in Rusham Lane Manchester - how Happy I am to read that my dear Sister Frances is so much better in Health; and in other respects I hope she is a very good Girl. If Sister Maria outstrips her in Bodily growth, Frances I doubt not, keeps pace in Mental qualifications. Sister Hannah must sup a good many Ale Possets yet before she is as tall as her

Brother John; he stands (in his Shoes) 5 Ft 7 In. and a proportionable breadth, (though by the bye not quite so broad as long); from what sister Maria tell me I judge Hannah to be as the saying here, "as fat as a lathe."

Whit Sunday

May 18:23

the Misses Williamsons of Fosters Wood I informed you in my last, I saw at Christmas; they promised me then they would write unto you; they Misses Brettargh's I saw about the same time; they complained of their inability, and want of something to say. I have not heard whether the Miss Birch's have received a letter or not, but I think if they had I should have heard. The Misses Ashworths I have not spoke to, this long while, in fact I have not seen them. Mrs. & Miss Hamilton have not call'd to see me this Age, and something or other has prevented me from calling upon them.

Well my dear Sister, I have not any News to tell you what would be gratifying, unless that I am in very good Health, and that your absence, and my dear Brothers' (not forgetting my dear Parents) endear you more than ever to my Affections, and how glad, as my dear little chatterer says, shall I be to see you, one day.

If my dear Mother does no, you ought to know better than eat Beer Possets; I dare say if I could hear, my Mother says, there was only a little Beer in it, nothing to do any harm, well, I will take it for granted it was so; I should love a Posset myself, of course; I could not wish to deprive you of one, but mind do not have Beer, but Buttermilk Possets. If my dear Maria /bless her/ is always healthy and Strong, Beer will soon change the Rosy Bloom of Health to pale faced Sickness; not that I suppose her to be a Tippler, but let me caution her against taking too many sly Sups from the can in the Bar, when Mother is not there. James & Joseph never taste such a thing, not them.

Sunday next is my Sunday out. I am going to see my Friend R. Knowles who has given me several invitations. Tell Dear Father Mr. Knowles has never received one letter from his Hand since your arrival in America. 'Tis strange we should both be thinking of the same subject at once; I did not forget the Anniversary of the day on which I last saw my dear Sisters & Brothers & Kind Mother, and it is with a tender feeling I remember the Affectionate parting & adieu with the best of Fathers.

Written along the left margin of the second page
I have scarce left room to assure you once more of my Kindest Love to each and every one of you, Hannah, Frances, Maria, Eliza, James & Joseph. 6 of the sweetest names in the world; how much I love you I cannot express.

adieu, adieu, repeats your Affect. Brother John Stott

This letter was written on two sides of a single sheet and contains no address for delivery. It must have been included in a larger Packet.

Nostalgia

For James, filled with sorrow that England was not yet able to embrace the reforms he so strongly advocated, exile would be bittersweet. These words, in the form of a song to which he made mention in Letter Seventeen, are testament to those sentiments.

The Voluntary Excile's Song in America, Nov. 19. 1821.
Oh, when shall I trod, where my forefathers trod,
And kneel, in the Church of my father, to God!

169

When shall I revisit my dear native soil?
The Island, devoted to sorrow, and Toil?

Oh! when shall I walk, in the Meadows so gay,
Where Hannah and I have together spread Hay;
When shall I revisit, the springs and the fountains,
I lov'd in my Youth, and the grey rocky mountains?

Oh when will despair, and bleak sorrow, and grief,
Raise up in the Land of my Mother, a chief,
Who will dash, in contempt of the statutes and pains,[a]
In the face of his Tyrants, their slave galling Chains?

Oh! when will the banners, of Liberty wave,
With star spangled Luster, o'er tyranny's grave;
When, will Hampden's[1] brave sons, the base Tyrants defy,
Under Liberty's banners, to conquer or die?

Oh! then I will tread, where my forefather's trod
And kneel, in the Church of my father to God,
Then, I will revisit, the springs and the fountains,
I lov'd in my youth, and the grey rocky mountains.

Oh! then, with the Heart of a patriot I'll fly,
And, with Liberty's banner, we'll conquer or die;
Fair freedom establish, in our native Isle,
And there, see the Loves and the Graces too, smile!

[a]alluding to the statute and penal Laws.

[1]*During the reform movement, a widespread network of agitation was developed in the form of clubs. One of those groups was the Hampden Club, probably first started in Royton in August of 1816. By the following March the number of Hampden Clubs*

had grown to 40 with the reformers claiming a membership of approximately 8000 in the Manchester area. Plans inaugurated by the various clubs were coordinated by delegates who traveled across the country promoting the cause of reform (Davis, "Lancashire Reformers 1816-1817" as referenced in Read 97-98).

Chapter VII
Afterword

The ways in which James, Hannah, John, Hannah, Frances, Maria, Eliza, James, and Joseph spent their remaining years were much less dramatic in a historical context, but may be of interest to the reader. To that end, a brief concluding biographical sketch of each Stott is presented.

James

While awaiting an opportunity to work as a surveyor, James served as the Head of Falls Academy near the Falls of Schuylkill. Finally, in 1828, James secured a position in his chosen field. He was employed in the Lehigh and Schuylkill fields as well as the Lackawanna and Susquehanna region, becoming one of the earliest mining engineers to locate coal in Northeastern Pennsylvania. James settled in Carbondale, Pennsylvania and after several years, Hannah and the children left the Philadelphia area to join him there.

From later correspondence with family members we know that James was well satisfied with his coal mining successes. In a letter written in 1830, James stated, "we now load about 86 wagons per week, and expect to load 100 wagons or 250 tons each week in a short time." He also mentioned his desire to "visit the coal mines in Nova Scotia and New Brunswick." Seemingly enchanted by his chosen profession, James described his mine's "subterraneous excavations" as if "lighted by a hundred Candles and supported by two hundred Pillars of Doric Order."

James' expertise must have been in great demand, often bringing more requests for his services than he could accommodate. Away from home on a mine surveying trip in 1837, James wrote to Hannah, "Mr. Livesley wanted me to prove his Coal for him at Black Creek but I declined, and Judge Coxe wishes me to find him Coal, but…I will come to you soon as ever I can - and return, if it please God to grant me Health and Strength to do these Things and others that are, and will be wanted."

Five years later, twenty-two years after leaving England, James' health and strength did decline. In 1842 at the age of sixty-four, he died in Carbondale. James Stott was an engineer, artist, author, teacher, and radical reformer. From his writings he revealed himself to be an eloquent, opinionated, principled, judgmental, impatient man who was also loving, deeply devoted to his wife and children, and totally committed to the cause of liberty.

Hannah

The author has experienced much disappointment in the fact that no personal writings by Hannah's could be found. All of our information about her comes from James and their children. Her opinions concerning the life choices made by James remains hidden.

It certainly takes little imagination to assume that, for Hannah, the years highlighted by this book were extremely difficult - from being left in England with young children and again pregnant, to embarking on an arduous ocean voyage followed by a relatively primitive lifestyle. In fact, it was not until the Stott's move to Carbondale in 1831 that conditions for Hannah became somewhat easier. In a letter dated October 15, 1830 from James to his son John, James asked John to, "tell your dear Mother that I have bought her a House (*in Carbondale*) (...) facing where I now live (...) it is thought (by many) the best Lot in the Village (...) Tell her further that she has been plagued for water these many years, but now she will have a fine stream of soft water at the foot of her Garden, and I am going to dig a well and fix a pump in one of the Cellars in order that she may have pure spring water without going out of Doors."

It was the house in Carbondale that was to become the Stott residence for the remainder of their lives. Although son James and daughter Frances made Carbondale their permanent home, other children married and lived elsewhere. According to existing correspondence, Hannah did travel to visit her children and grandchildren. During her lifetime, she experienced the death of a daughter (Mary) at age six, a son (John) at age thirty-two, and possibly another son (Joseph) of whom little is known after the age of seventeen.

Hannah outlived her husband by eight years, her death occurring on August 30, 1850. There is some question as to how well Hannah was able to read and write. The existence of correspondence from every member of the family except Hannah certainly brings the level of her education into question. Clearly, she must have been strong, resourceful, flexible, and a devoted mother and wife. There is much evidence that she was greatly admired by her husband and was the recipient of many expressions of his love. That she left no direct evidence of her true character, outlook, and beliefs is both sad and understandable for the time.

John

John, at the conclusion of his apprenticeship with Mr. Goadsby in England, emigrated to America. The year of his arrival is uncertain. From the letters addressed to him, we know that it occurred somewhere between 1823 and 1827.

John chose to settle in Manayunk in Philadelphia County, a village established by those wishing to make use of the water power derived from the Flat Rock Canal - part of the Schuylkill chain. The first mill had been built in 1819 and by 1832 there were fourteen mills and over 400 homes (Gordon [a] p.272). Thus, John became a druggist in Manayunk just as it was experiencing rapid growth.

On January 1, 1828, John married Matilda Nicholas who died ten months later either in childbirth or shortly thereafter. Their daughter Eliza survived. Following her death, James penned a letter to John urging him to consider relocating to Carbondale as the community was dissatisfied with "drug and medical line" services and had an expected population increase of "not less than 500 working men" by next season. James stated, "if you could sell out your establishment and come up here in early spring, perhaps it would in the end be for the best." John, however, decided to remain in the Philadelphia area.

There is evidence that John enrolled in medical school. On January 30, 1831, James wrote John a note excusing him for not writing "on account that you are so busy studying and digesting your Lectures." Further, James stated, "I would rather see you a first-rate apothecary and Druggist than a set-at-naught Physician (...). In order to this you must have your mind undivided, and bring the whole strength of your mental faculties to bear upon the subject you wish to acquire; when Lectures are over you must compare notes, read such authors, and endeavour to gain such knowledge as the different professors have pointed out to you; and in any doubtful case, during the recess, I would wait upon them and ask their advice, or beg an explanation." Later in the letter, James wrote, "I do earnestly advise you not to study the Science of Love anymore, until you have got a Professor's Knowledge of the Science of Medicine."

Whether or not John ever had the opportunity to begin his medical practice has not been discovered. We do know that in June of 1834 he was married for a second time to a woman named Mary. Sadly, two years later in 1836, John died at the age of thirty-two.

Hannah

Hannah, James and Hannah's eldest daughter, remained in Philadelphia with her mother and siblings while her father was establishing his career in Carbondale. At the beginning of that time, in 1828, she opened a school for girls and for young boys under the age of six. The school was located in the home of her brother John in Manayunk.

It was also during her father's absence, that Hannah was apparently suffering the distresses of an unrequited "love affair" with a man we know only as "Mr. U." Having heard about Hannah's plight, her father wrote to John asking him to help his sister bear her sorrow. In the letter to John, James stated, "We have concluded that she (*Hannah*) has mUsic imprinted in her memory, she writes the big U so often in her letter. 'Mr. U. looked fairer then etc.' 'Mr. U and I etc.' 'Mr. U had a party etc.' 'Mr. U talked to Mother etc.' 'Mr. U and Mother and I went etc.' 'Mr. U wishes etc.' In all she mentions the big U about thirteen times; what do you think of it John? don't you think she has been studying mUsick? (...) an experienced hand can better bear such ills, and thole the scorn. Comfort her, John, comfort your Sister, and if you too are sick? why then mingle your Tears in the same Lachyrmatory and keep each other's Secret."

Whatever Hannah's feelings for the mysterious "Mr. U," she was also acquainted with an English gentleman named James Birdsall. He had been born near Leeds, Yorkshire, England in 1800. After learning the woolen business from his father, he emigrated to the United States in 1825. First sorting wool in Boston, he left for Philadelphia arriving in time to meet Hannah in 1827 or 1828. Love must have convinced him to abandon Philadelphia because when Hannah moved with her parents to Carbondale, James Birdsall followed. They were married shortly thereafter on August 1, 1831.

During the first years of their marriage, Hannah and James Birdsall lived in Carbondale. James tried several lines of work before returning to the woolen business. While traveling in 1837, James Stott wrote to his daughter, Hannah, "I would gently hint if James B. will allow me, that he should be extremely Careful this summer how he carries on - above all things mind and not run into debt.... it is almost certain that this will be the worst Season for Tradesmen both here and in England that there has been in twenty years."

Finally in 1844, James was able to open a roll carding and cloth finishing shop on what is now Eighth Avenue. At that time, most of the woolen goods in Carbondale were made in people's homes. James' new venture was welcomed as it removed some of the more arduous steps from the home weavers while assuring the townspeople of a better finished product. His success in Carbondale encouraged James to start his own woolen mill in the small settlement of Seelyville, east of Carbondale. In 1846, he established his mill (Birdsall 1-6), and he and Hannah built their home across the road.

Hannah and James were the parents of six children, William, James Charles, Elizabeth, Hannah Maria, Emma, and George. Elizabeth and Hannah Maria died when they were very young children - aged two and three years, respectively, and Emma died in childbirth. Son William never married. George married Amanda Van Kuren. Their daughter Grace, married to Fred Staph, had no children.

It was James Charles who eventually assumed responsibility for the operation of the woolen mill. He decided to construct a larger dwelling close to that of his parents for he, his wife Margaret Woodward, and their growing family. Their three surviving daughters remained single and continued to live in that second Birdsall home until the mid-nineteen hundreds. Son Willard James inherited the mill and kept it operational until his retirement in 1951 when it was sold and subsequently closed.

Hannah died on March 16, 1883 at the age of seventy-five.

Frances

There is no evidence that Frances married. She lived in Carbondale with James, Jr. throughout her lifetime. Although she was often in ill health as a child, she did reach the age of fifty-five, dying on November 6, 1865.

Maria

Maria married Daniel Gore Bailey on June 1, 1841. They had four children whom they named Anna, James, Frank, and Alice. Both Frank and James died when they were young. Anna married F. C. Lowthrope and Alice married William Matthews. Alice and William had a son named William and then, sadly, Alice died giving birth to their second son, Robert. (Alice's husband William married three more times, his second and third wives also dying in childbirth).

Records show that Maria's death occurred on March 16, 1886 in Trenton, New Jersey. She was seventy-three years of age.

Eliza

Eliza had two gentlemen interested in marrying her, William Griffith and Archibald B. Hackley. On May 28, 1834, Eliza married Archibald B. Hackley. According to family history, "Willie" was so upset that he fled to Paris in an attempt to mend his broken heart. In 1836, while living in Unadilla, New York, Eliza gave birth to son Charles Elihu. Sadly, Archibald passed away in February of 1837 leaving Eliza alone with an infant son to raise.

Concerned about his daughter Eliza, James wrote on November 15, 1837, "I wish her (*Fanny*) to tell Eliza that I will send her money (Ten Dollars) to pay Coach fare if she will come and spend the winter with us." Whether Eliza and son Charles did in fact travel to Carbondale is uncertain. We do know that a short time later Willie Griffith returned from France and asked Eliza for her hand in marriage. Eliza agreed and shortly thereafter became Willie's wife.

Eliza's son Charles became a physician and served in that capacity during the Civil War. During the war his battlefield surgical instruments were stolen along with his horse, both to later be returned to him. Those instruments remain in the author's family. Charles was married to Emma Kent, and they were the parents of two sons, Kent and Charles James, and a daughter, Mary. It was Mary who first transcribed a portion of the Stott letters as well as collated many of the drawings and memorabilia.

Eliza lived to see her son, Charles return safely from the War. She died on June 6, 1874.

James, Jr.

Very little information is available on James' life. It is known that, on September 10, 1871, at age fifty-four, he married Mary Fordham Baker. She was the widow of a Charles Baker and the mother of two daughters. James and Mary had no children of their own. He continued to live in the Stott house in Carbondale until his death. Inheriting his father's talent for sketching, some of his drawings of the Pennsylvania countryside have fortunately been preserved.

Joseph

Joseph moved with his mother, Hannah, to Carbondale at age eleven. In 1837, at age seventeen, Joseph wrote the following in a letter to his sister, Hannah. "Mother told Sam Cox to see Doctor Smith and ask him if he would undertake to cure me." Further, Joseph remarked, "that the Dr. would be willing for me to board with him but could not tell if he could cure me or not untill he saw my Leg." The nature of Joseph's problem is not known nor do we have any information as to whether he found a cure. A letter to James from a nephew in England near the end of 1840 made mention of the death of John and of Eliza's husband, but said nothing to indicate that Joseph had succumbed to his illness. No date for his death has been found by the author.

The information contained in this *Afterward* was obtained from Stott letters, oral histories, family Bibles, and family genealogy searches. Descendants of James and Hannah may have access to further data.

THE STOTT FAMILY

Stephen Stott
born about 1752
Middleton, Lancashire, England

Married Frances in 1803
St. Leonard's Church, Middleton, England

Thomas   Stephen   William   **James**
born March 20, 1778
Middleton , England

died October 3, 1842
Carbondale, PA

(Stephen and Frances Stott may have had daughters. In his letters,
James refers to "sisters," but it unclear whether
they are, in fact, siblings or wives of his brothers.)

In 1804 **James** married **Hannah** Crossley

Hannah Crossley
born June 24, 1780
Yorkshire, England
died August 30, 1850
Carbondale, PA

Children of **James** and **Hannah Stott**

John b. March 24, 1804   **Mary** b. June, 1806   **Hannah** b. July 25, 1808
d. December 3, 1836   d. August 4, 1812   d. March 16, 1883

Frances b. September 10, 1810   **Maria** b. March 12, 1813
d. November 6, 1865   d. March 16, 1886

Eliza b. August 12, 1815   **James** b. November 1817
d. June 6, 1874   d. date unknown

Joseph b. July 3, 1820
d. date unknown

RELATIONSHIP OF JAMES STOTT TO THE AUTHOR

James and Hannah's daughter, **Hannah**
married James Birdsall
August 1, 1831

Hannah Stott and James Birdsall

Elizabeth   Hannah   Emma

William   **James Charles**   George
b. 1836 d. 1920

James Charles Birdsall married Margaret Woodward

Charles   Isabel   Minnie   Mattie   George

Fannie   Alice   Emma   Bertha

Willard James
b. 1879 d. 1976

Willard James Birdsall married Elizabeth Grace Ham

Robert Wallace   **Margaret Elizabeth**
b. 1909 d. 2004

Margaret Elizabeth Birdsall married David Joseph Brunn

Barbara Eda   **Susan Foster**
b. 1939

Susan Foster Brunn (author) married J. David Puett

David Wilson   Michael James

David Wilson Puett married Mary Timko

Brannon Foster   Andrew Connor   Margaret Grace

Illustrations

Photograph taken of an oil portrait of James Stott. It is not known who created the original painting nor when it was done.

*Photograph taken of an oil portrait of Hannah Stott. The artist and date
of the original painting are not known.*

James Stott's business card used while he was still residing in England.

Watercolor depicting Whitehorse Tavern found by the author in a folder containing numerous drawings and paintings by James Stott. This was probably the sketch to which James referred in Letter Twenty.

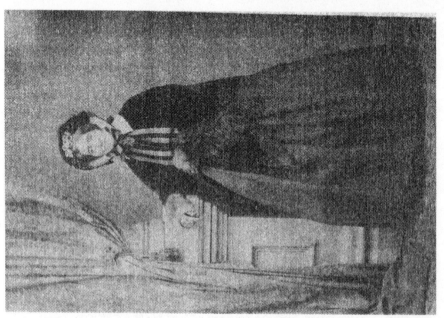

Eliza S. Griffeth
Feb. 1864

Pictures of three of James and Hannah's daughters. The author was unable to locate any photographs of Maria or her brothers.

Copy of the first page of Letter Two transcribed in this volume.

It is said to be the Longest upon the Keel, the best built, and the handsomest Vessel in the World — its Length is 165 feet between Decks — it has been built by a Dutchman, it certainly is the most beautiful Ship I ever saw, between Decks looks almost large enough to hold a little Village — the Stem of the Vessel is adorned with a Bust of the Great Hercules, most beautifully carved, shewing Defiance in his Eyes, over his Shoulders hang the Skin of the Nemean Lion — I then went on Board the Washington which built 74, which is now laid up in ordinary — we were very complaisantly shewn throughout, the Captains, State Room and &c. by one of the Lieutenants — every part of her was admirably clean and regular. I forgot to say, above, that the name of the new Ship (which is the pride of Columbia) is the Ohio, she is called after one of the western States, — notwithstanding the various Stories you have heard about the haughtiness of the Americans, I assure you I have met with nothing but the greatest civility during the short time I have been on Shore — This Day a Merchant of the City whom I accidentally fell into conversation with upon the Quay, invited me to Dinner, after which he very condescendingly offered to shew me through the Navy Yard — he insisted upon paying all Expences — we crossed the River in a Steam Boat, and recrossed it in one propelled along by Horses, a thing which I never heard of in England — He gave me an account of the State of Trade, which he represents as flat and dull at present, but I believe from his account that Trade is not so bad as it is in England by a great deal — every working man is paid I had most said overpaid, for his Labour — even a woman, who is a good [illegible] Shop will earn five or six dollars per week — that is from 40 to 48 New York Shillings — The Natives of this Country as far as I know at present are remarkably good Workmen — the Mechanics of almost all descriptions may come over from England to learn — particularly Iron founders, Brass founders, Tin plate workers, engravers, watchmakers, Tailors, Shoemakers, &c. &c. Farming is the best Trade followed even in the neighbourhood of this City where Land I am told is high — but before I write again I will get Particulars upon the Subject — Horses are remarkably fine clean limbed Creatures in this City — I am told there is not a greased Horse in the whole State — I have not yet learned the price of Provisions generally, in this country, suffice it to say, all are good and plentiful — there is a capital Market place in this City, which is well supplied with every thing, every Day in the week, Cherries, fine Apples, Lemons, Oranges, Lemons, Raspberries, Strawberries, Potatoes, Colly flowers, Kidney Beans, Cabbages and a many sorts of Greens unknown in England — [illegible] may be shewn to my Friends [illegible] I mean you [illegible] only for the [illegible] of my [illegible] Children and I [illegible] from this Paper or my [illegible]

Second page of Letter Two transcribed in this volume.

Announcement of the opening of the school established by James Stott and mentioned in Letter Thirteen.

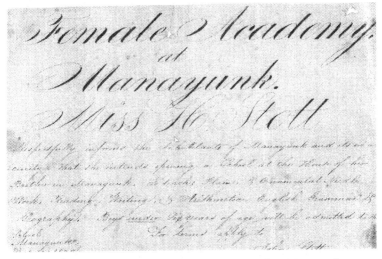

Notice of the school that daughter Hannah started in Manayunk,
Pennsylvania shortly before moving to Carbondale.

Sketch created by James Stott's son, James, at age twelve.

Paragraph in James Stott's handwriting and apparently created by him in April, 1820.

Bibliography

Bamford, Samuel. *Passages in the Life of a Radical.* Oxford University Press, Oxford, 1984 (first published by Messrs Simpkin, Marshall, London, 1844).

Beales, Derek. *From Castlereagh to Gladston 1815-1885.* W.W. Norton & Company, Inc., New York, 1969.

Birdsall, R. W. *History of Birdsall Brothers Company 1844 - 1927.* The Sterling Press, New York (undated publication).

Brinton, Crane, Christopher, John B., and Wolff, Robert Lee. *A History of Civilization Volume Two: 1715 to the Present.* 2nd Edition, Prentice Hall, Inc. Englewood Cliffs, New Jersey, 1955, 1960.

Cobbett, William. *A Journal of a Year's Residence in the United States of America.* Southern Illinois University Press, Carbondale, Illinois, 1964.

Dangerfield, George. *The Era of Good Feelings.* Ivan R. Dee Inc., Chicago, Illinois, 1989 (originally published by Harcourt, Brace and Company, 1952).

Davis, H. W. C., "Lancashire Reformers 1816 - 17." Bulletin of the John Rylands Library, Vol. 10, 1926, and separately. Footnoted in *Peterloo The Massacre and its Background,* by Donald Read, p. 98.

Edwards, J. R. *British History 1815 - 1939*. Humanities Press, New York, 1970.

Family Search, Film Number 458547, Family History Library, Salt Lake City, Utah.

Gordon, Thomas, F. [a]. *Gazetteer of the State of Pennsylvania*. T. Belknap, Philadelphia, 1832.

Gordon. Thomas F. [b]. *Gazetteer of the State of New Jersey*. Daniel Fenton, Trenton, New Jersey, 1834. Reprinted Polyanthos, Inc. Cottonport, Louisiana, 1973.

Halevy, Elie. Trans. E. I. Watkin *A History of the English People 1815-1830*. Harcourt, Brace & Company, New York, 1924.

Lankevich, George J. *American Metropolis A History of New York City*. New York University Press, New York, 1998.

Nattrass, Leonora. *William Cobbett: The Politics of Style*. Cambridge University Press, Cambridge, 1995.

Palmer, R. R. and Colton Joel. *A History of the Modern World*. Alfred A. Knopf, New York, 1956.

Passenger List, Ship Warren, M-425, Roll 31, List #058 - Jan. 4-Dec. 24, 1821, National Archives, Washington, D.C.

Passenger Lists, Microfiche Film 0002246, Family History Library, Salt Lake City, Utah.

Read, Donald. *Peterloo, The "Massacre" and Its Background*. Manchester University Press, Manchester, England, 1958.

Rickword, Edgell, Editor. *Radical Squibs & Loyal Ripostes, Satirical Pamphlets of the Regency Period, 1819-1821.* Adams & Dart, Somerset, England, 1971.

Rosenwaike, Ira. *Population History of New York City.* Syracuse University Press, Syracuse New York, 1972.

Trevelyan, George Macaulay. *British History in the Nineteenth Century (1782-1901).* Longmans, Green and Co. London, England, 1933.